PRAISE FOR PHIL EARLE:

'P
LI
WI
TH

'A

'LI

TI
NA

'P
F
FE

'PI
TI
S
TH
FO

'PI
W

'I

'

WONDERFULLY REAL STORY' – KEVIN BROOKS

'PHIL

ABOUT I

IL
R
Y.
ER
D
E'
M

N

E,
CK

E
I.
AN

I.'
IL'
IES

ES
AY

T'
IZIE

A

ENSITIVELY
-TURNING NOVEL.
ACQUELINE WILSON

PHIL EARLE was born and raised in the great city of Hull. His first job was as a care worker in a children's home, which inspired him to train as a drama therapist. After a couple of years in the care sector, Phil chose the more sedate lifestyle of a bookseller, and now spends his time writing children's books as well as selling them for a publisher.

Phil lives on a hill in south-east London with his family, and writes on the bus to work. No one has used this as an excuse to pinch his laptop. Yet.

www.philearle.com
Twitter: @philearle#bubblewrapboy

Books by Phil Earle

BEING BILLY
THE BUBBLE WRAP BOY
HEROIC
SAVING DAISY

THE BUBBLE WRAP BOY

WRAP

BOY

PHIL EARLE

PENGUIN BOOKS

PENGUIN BOOKS

Published by the Penguin Group
Penguin Books Ltd, 80 Strand, London WC2R ORL, England
Penguin Group (USA) Inc., 375 Hudson Street, New York, New York 10014, USA
Penguin Group (Canada), 90 Eglinton Avenue East, Suite 700, Toronto, Ontario, Canada M4P 2Y3
(a division of Pearson Penguin Canada Inc.)
Penguin Ireland, 25 St Stephen's Green, Dublin 2, Ireland (a division of Penguin Books Ltd)
Penguin Group (Australia), 707 Collins Street, Melbourne, Victoria 3008, Australia
(a division of Pearson Australia Group Pty Ltd)
Penguin Books India Pvt Ltd, 11 Community Centre, Panchsheel Park, New Delhi – 110 017, India
Penguin Group (NZ), 67 Apollo Drive, Rosedale, Auckland 0632, New Zealand
(a division of Pearson New Zealand Ltd)
Penguin Books (South Africa) (Pty) Ltd, Block D, Rosebank Office Park,
181 Jan Smuts Avenue, Parktown North, Gauteng 2193, South Africa

Penguin Books Ltd, Registered Offices: 80 Strand, London WC2R ORL, England

www.penguin.com

First published 2014
003

Set in 10.5/15.5pt Sabon LT Std
Made and printed in England by Clays Ltd, St Ives plc

British Library Cataloguing in Publication Data
A CIP catalogue record for this book is available from the British Library

ISBN: 978-0-141-34629-8

www.greenpenguin.co.uk

Penguin Books is committed to a sustainable
future for our business, our readers and our planet.
This book is made from Forest Stewardship
Council™ certified paper.

*This book is dedicated to my friends Shannon
Cullen and Becky Stradwick, who didn't laugh
(or groan) when I asked for a favour . . .*

There's a saying that I hate.

I know it shouldn't bother me like it does, because it's only a saying.

A sentence.

Six words. Five of which are one syllable long.

I'm sure there are more irritating phrases; in fact I know there are.

For example, my skin itches every time Sinus hides his hideous lack of tact behind his beloved:

You'd rather hear it than be deaf . . .

Or my late, great, flatulent granddad's only pearl of wisdom:

Pull my finger . . .

Believe me, if he ever uttered those fateful words to you in an enclosed space it was time to leave. Quickly.

The reason I hate this *other* saying so much is because of the number of times it's rolled out in front of me, like the heavenly answer to my (to date) underwhelming existence.

Good things come in small packages.

OK, it's out there, burning my throat with vom at its very utterance. But at least I don't have to say it again.

Have you ever heard a twee-er, glibber, more patronizing sentence in your life?

What does it mean? It has no substance, no sub-text, nothing.

All it is is a gargantuan, ironic pat on the head from people who *really* want to tell you that your life as a short-arse is going to be packed with woe and anguish.

Come on, people. If that's what you're thinking then give it to me straight. I have broad shoulders (for my size).

I reconciled myself to my height, or massive lack of it, long ago. Long before I started secondary school and couldn't reach my locker, well before being mistaken for a nursery kid as I started my final year of primary.

It's how it's always been, no alarms and no surprises.

When I look in the mirror I see a short kid, or the top of a short kid's head anyway.

And I think I'd deal with it even better if people didn't keep ramming *that* sentence down my throat.

I've heard it so often in the last two years that I've started obsessing over it, trying to prove the theory wrong with cold hard facts.

I want to blow their lame words clean out the water and say (in the ridiculous squeaky voice that came with my stupidly small body) . . .

'HA! SEE?? I will always be a clumsy feckless failure, not the "big" package you claim I am.'

Let me give you an example. In fact, let me give you loads of them.

Here's a carousel of famous small people, and all of them, *deeply* flawed.

Henri de Toulouse-Lautrec (1864–1901)

Painter, printmaker, innovator, short-arse.

So short was his arse that he turned to alcohol to drown his sorrows, inventing a lethal cocktail called 'The Earthquake', which he took to hiding in his specially adapted walking cane.

By the age of twenty-nine he was pickled in booze and rife with unseemly disease, and by the age of thirty-six, well, he was dead.

Toulouse was one of the success stories – at least he left behind the legacy of his work, unlike this next mob.

Genghis Khan, Pol Pott, Stalin, Mussolini, Hitler: a collection of tyrants not bettered in ancient or modern history, and not one of them more than five foot nine inches high.

Talk about *small-man syndrome.*

Made me wonder (for like a millisecond) about whether I should consider a life in politics. They might have been hideous tyrants, but I bet they were tyrants with women hanging off them. And I don't mean their mothers. Mind you, I bet Genghis's mum was easier-going than mine.

It's not just historical short dudes who were rubbish either. Look around now and it's hard to find a positive role model, I mean:

Tom Cruise (nose)
Prince ('The Purple Perv'? They'd never have dared call him that if he'd been taller)

Diego Maradona (single-handedly cheated England out of the 1986 World Cup)

The Ewoks (ruined what would have been the best movie trilogy of all time)

I could go on, fill another page or two at least, but you'd get the wrong idea about me. I'm not bitter. It might read like it, but I'm not, honest.

When opportunity comes my way, I try to take it.

Even if that means grabbing the nearest stepladder and leaning precariously from the very top rung. If that's what it takes, then fine – I'm up for it.

My problem is that every time I try, every time I reach up and try something new, the stepladder topples over in the most public way possible, and I topple with it.

The bruises might fade, but my reputation doesn't.

To everyone who knows me I'm Tiny Charlie from the Chinese chippy. Clumsy, klutzy Charlie Han, who should know better, but never learns.

And that's the bit that stings way worse than being labelled a short-arse.

Because if there's a saying I *do* believe in, it's this:

Everyone's good at something.

I do believe that.

I do.

I have to.

Because the alternative just isn't worth thinking about.

All I have to do is work out what my *something* is.

The thing that turns me from an ewok to . . . I don't know, Yoda?

Yep, Yoda. I'd settle for that in a second. A millisecond even.

Despite the ears. Despite the green.

So that's it. Until I find my thing, I'm channelling one hundred per cent pure unadulterated Yoda.

Find it I must. My calling it is.

Note to self. Drop the Yoda speak. Girls won't go for it.

I breathed deeply, nerves prickling beneath my costume.

'Don't be a clown,' I told myself. It wasn't the most demanding role, after all. No time on stage with Romeo *or* Juliet, no lines or interaction either, well, apart from with the lifeless body of Mercutio as I dragged him off stage. Couldn't imagine I'd be troubling the reviewers with the complexity of my performance.

I waited for Matty Dias to stop milking Mercutio's death, reckoning my birthday would come around by the time he stopped writhing about, calling for his mummy (I didn't remember *that* bit in the original text).

I wasn't jealous of him though. I hadn't expected to find my name next to a main part when I ducked through people's legs to spy the cast list pinned to the notice board. It would've been a brave move to give a part to someone who sounded like they were addicted to helium.

I'd hoped to bag a part with a name though, rather than just *Body Dragger Number Two*. I'd run to the library to see what the script said it involved, but couldn't find a reference anywhere. Even Google threw up a blank. I knew then that it was going to be the bittiest bit-part, the sort they offer up to the special kids, you know, just so they feel involved. There seemed little point in begging for promotion to *BD Number One* ...

It didn't take me long to get over it; it was a foot in the door, after all. A stepping stone.

I just had to make sure I didn't fall over it.

As the lights finally dimmed on Mercutio, I adjusted my hat (which, like every bit of my costume, was way too big) and strode purposefully to centre stage. Wiping a single imaginary tear from my cheek (my own exquisite addition to the role), I gripped the fallen warrior underneath the shoulders and leaned back, expecting his body to slide across the stage, just like it had in the dress rehearsal.

Except nothing moved.

I pulled harder, my body arching further, yet it was like Mercutio had been replaced by the deadest of weights.

Whispers started to roll from the audience, followed by chuckles that only grew louder with every useless tug I made.

'What are you doing?' hissed the resurrected corpse.

'Aren't you meant to be dead?' I squeaked back quietly, though it must have come out as a stage whisper as the first four rows all heard me, heads thrown back as they laughed.

I tried to work out what was stopping us, finally catching sight of his sword, wedged between floorboards, pinning him to the stage.

'It's your sword, it's –'

'Just pull, you idiot!'

So I did, and after several monumental efforts the blade finally dislodged itself, sending both the corpse and me skidding backwards across the stage.

7

I fought to stay upright, but with Mercutio's weight on top of me I delivered the most ungraceful dance ever witnessed on the British stage. The Royal Ballet it wasn't.

There was a gasp from the audience as we thudded against a pillar, the biggest reaction there'd been all evening, and for a split second I wondered if I'd accidentally created a bit of *real* theatre.

But then I felt the pillar wobble behind me, accelerating quickly into a tilt. You see, the pillar was actually a pretty pivotal bit of the set, beneath Juliet's balcony, so if it fell, well, the odds were the balcony would too . . .

Matty Dias was well ahead of me in his structural assessment, fully alive now as he ran, screaming, for the wings.

I followed him quickly as the pillar hurtled towards the floor, watching in horror as the balcony started to shake.

To make it worse, the stage lights were now back up, ready for the next scene. I saw Romeo (Robbie Bootle – school's most popular student) stride centre stage, lost in his own grief, completely unaware that if the balcony fell he'd be the next person to be mourned.

I had to do something, so dashed behind the balcony to see the entire set lurching precariously forward. The stage weights holding it all in place were rapidly becoming dislodged, the main rope that anchored it at the middle unravelling cartoon style.

Without thinking, I sprinted for the rope and leapt on it. If I could re-tether it, then everything would hold still and Romeo wouldn't die quite yet or quite as literally.

It was the right idea – of course it was. At least it was if you were of normal size and weight. But my impact on the rope was minimal, like a fly landing on an elephant, hoping to stop him from thundering on.

Within a second I knew it wasn't going to work, and as the balcony whooshed forward and I impersonated Tarzan on a vine, it was clear I could save either myself or the hapless Romeo. I may not be a coward, but I'm not an idiot either. With one final graceless movement I crumpled to the ground, shouting as I fell.

'Jump, Romeo! Jump!!'

I doubted he heard me above the cacophonous din created by the tumbling timber and three hundred terrified audience members.

All I could do was roll into a ball and hope for the best.

The fair city of Verona looked more like the battlefields of Iraq.

Splintered scenery jutted from the floor at unusual angles, the stage lights swung perilously over the audience, highlighting that the damage wasn't restricted to the set.

There in the front row of the audience, spread-eagled on the laps of the Lord and Lady Mayor, lay the lovestruck Romeo, his chin savaged by the medal on the dignitary's chain of office.

No one moved at first, not even me (though I allowed myself to gasp for air in relief). The mayor's wife had taken the brunt of the blow, but showed little sign of emotion. She simply sat there, frozen, hand suspended in the air, still clutching her bag of Maltesers. Robbie had a lot to thank her love of chocolate balls for. It had gifted him the softest of landings.

His head wasn't quite so cushioned. The ceremonial chain had gouged a jagged hole in his chin that was spraying blood all over the mayor's robes. Mum would have had a fit if she'd seen it. Blood was murder to shift, apparently.

I wandered to the front of the stage, leaning forward as I asked, 'You all right, Robbie?'

'Drop the curtain!' came the cry from the wings, which might have made me giggle if I hadn't been in *so* much trouble.

It was a bit late for that. Thirty square metres of red velvet was nowhere near enough to hide this carnage, not unless they were going to drape it over the audience as well.

The curtain fell anyway, swooshing into me with such force that it almost knocked me on top of Robbie too. Fighting its folds as it enveloped me, I decided now might be the right time for a sharp exit. It wouldn't take anyone long to put two and two together and spell *Charlie Han*.

I scuttled, crab-like, towards the wings, head down, best 'Not guilty, m'lud' face plastered on, but just as my feet hit the shadows my own name assaulted my eardrums.

It should've been a moment, *the* moment, the one to define me – after all, I'd dreamed of Carly Stoneham calling my name since the start of year seven.

Although in those fantasies she was calling it playfully, with a chuckle, as if I'd said something dazzling and witty.

She certainly wasn't bellowing it at me, every letter packed tight with rattlesnake venom.

I think it's fair to say she wasn't in character any more, unless Juliet actually turned out to be a kick-ass hit girl, hell-bent on avenging Romeo's minor chin wound.

She still looked fit, though, even if her immaculate braided hair was as big a casualty as Robbie. Incandescent rage clearly suited her.

'What did you do that for?' she yelled.

'Do what?' I hoped she was as forgiving as she was fit.

'Let go of the rope like that! You knew it was anchoring the balcony in place.'

My cheeks flushed in shame. 'I couldn't help it. The weight of it was lifting me up. If I hadn't let go, I'd have ended up in the gods.'

'Well, rather that than let it fall on Robbie. If he hadn't been so athletic, it would have crushed him.'

'He's all right, though, isn't he?' I cringed at the sight of him, chin still erupting. 'He's a centre forward – diving's second nature.'

My lame attempt at humour was met by a volcanic look.

'No, he's not all right. He'll probably have to go to A&E for stitches and the mayor's gown will need dry-cleaning. Miss has cancelled the play and now I'm never going to get off with him, am I?'

I felt for her, really I did. So much so that without a thought for myself I volunteered to save the day by taking on Robbie's part. But when that resulted in other cast members having to restrain Carly from me, I realized I'd learned Robbie's lines in vain.

Still, it wouldn't be a waste. I could regurgitate them in an exam soon enough. Learning Mercutio's speeches as well might have been overkill, though I'd done it with the most honourable of intentions. He was a funny guy, quick with the rapier wit. If I was the fair Juliet, I might get tired of Romeo's wailing and let his best mate cop a feel instead.

By the time I shook myself out of that blissfully naive headspace, Carly had been replaced by the less fair Mrs Gee, who was clearly as unimpressed as Carly, sharing the view that Romeo's wellbeing was more important than mine.

'Why are you always so clumsy?' she roared. 'I trusted you, Charlie. Surely you realized that letting go of the rope was a terrible idea?'

I was quickly getting the picture: catapulting the short kid into space was better than injuring the talent. I made a note to remember that in the future.

'Maybe I should get out from under your feet, miss?' I offered. 'Looks like I've done enough damage.'

I could feel daggers being drawn from tights all across the stage. Knew that even if they didn't reach their target tonight, there was always tomorrow: plenty of time for me to do the walk of shame. Again.

'Oh, I don't think so. I can hardly expect the others to tidy up the mess you've created, especially after all their creativity has resulted in *nothing*. The show might not be going on, but the party can, and don't you think about joining us until the stage is clear. In fact, it might be best if you don't think about it at all.'

She strode off like a leading lady herself, squeezing a weepy-looking Carly as she went, leaving me to drown under a tidal wave of déjà vu.

I cursed as I pushed the broom around. At their stupidity as much as mine. I mean, who in their right mind gives a job based on strength to the smallest kid in the school's history?

The others stalked past, warning me on Robbie's behalf, flicking filthy looks, sarcastic comments and, to really strike the fear of living god into me, the occasional dead arm. Worse would follow. It always did.

I tried to look at it positively: some of them had threatened me by name. This was progress; at least they knew who I was for once, rather than simply 'the Chinese midget'.

The broom sat heavily in my hands, and my mood didn't improve when the debris around me seemed to get bigger rather than smaller. Who'd have thought one little trip could do so much damage?

By the time I'd swept the last of the set into the forty-fifth bin bag, I wasn't really in the party mood and, anyway, from what I could hear it sounded like a pretty flat do. No celebrating or cheering – it was so quiet all you could hear were cheese puffs being munched through clenched jaws.

Should I risk it? Show my face and say sorry? I could see their expressions, scrunched up and angry, desperate to make me do *the walk* now while their anger was at its freshest. I could almost see their legs twitching, ready for the first swing, feel my own shins echo in pain. It wasn't like I didn't know what to expect.

If that was on the agenda for tonight, then I'd give it a miss. Take my chances and hope they'd cool off. There was a first time for everything.

I stepped outside to something I wasn't expecting.

A round of applause.

Well, I say a round, but that would involve more than one person doing the clapping.

And of course there wasn't. There was just one.

My friend. Sinus.

Who neatly leads me back to another saying:

You can't choose your family, but you can choose your friends.

It's the sort of saying that makes me want to ram my head through a reinforced wall. Whoever came up with that little gem had never walked a day in my size threes.

Choice, you see, hasn't ever come into it. It's not like I've spent the last nine years of school casing out the playground, scratching my chin and thinking, Yes, today I will be friends with you and you and most certainly not YOU.

Nice idea, but never going to happen. That sort of choice only belongs to other, normal people.

And that's why Sinus and I gravitated towards each other and became friends.

Well, I say 'friends'.

I think that's what he is. We've never exactly talked about what our hanging out means. It just kind of happened. We stood together so many times – in games lessons, in the playground, the last to be picked on every occasion – that eventually we ended up kind of joined. Like a couple of lepers.

I'm not sure if real friendship is based on stuff like this, but I liked him.

Kind of.

He didn't sneer at me or find new and exotic ways of insulting my height; he didn't jump on me as I piled things into my locker (sympathetically placed on the bottom row to maximize the gag). I had trainer marks tattooed into my back these days: standing on the short kid was an Olympic sport and *everyone* wanted that gold medal.

The first thing I noticed after the clapping stopped was of course Sinus's downfall, the thing that relegated him to the losers' third division alongside me.

THE NOSE.

I haven't left the caps lock on by accident – there's no way you could ever refer to the monstrosity that sat between his cheeks in lower case. It just wouldn't do it justice.

THE NOSE was so long, so hooked and yet so bulbous that it defined him entirely. When people talked about it, their voices would rise in volume as their own caps lock kicked in. Old people would gape as he walked down the street; young kids hide themselves in the folds of their mothers' skirts rather than face the deformity that was Sinus's nose.

In short, his nose made me relieved to be a mere short-arse. There was always a tiny chance that I might grow, but his nose was never going to shrink. Maybe that's why I put up with him, because he had to do the *walk of shame* as often as I did.

His name didn't help him either.

Linus Sedgley.

Innocent at first, but add in the hooter and it was a gift to the bullies. Linus very quickly became Sinus, and the name stuck firmer than a fossilized bogey under a desk.

Everyone called him that, kids *and* teachers. He showed me his school report once and you could see that three different teachers had used Tippex at the start of his name to hide their error. Old Man Gash, the English teacher, didn't even bother to correct himself, just wrote openly about the lack of drive that Sinus showed in lessons.

If the label bothered him, he didn't show it. If anything, he adopted it. Texts were always signed off with his nickname, cards too, so I never called him anything but Sinus. That's who he was.

He was waiting for me against the theatre wall, a shadow of his profile thrown huge against the bricks. It was eerie, like an American eagle waiting to pick me off.

Fortunately, before the fear really kicked in, he spoke, breaking the tension.

'Bravo!' he yelled. 'Encore. Encore.' Unsurprisingly, he spoke through his nose, nostrils flaring like a racehorse as he pushed out every word.

'Yeah, yeah, whatever.' I made to walk on like I was angry, but he followed, playfully slapping me on the back.

'No, really. It was awesome. Once everyone wiped the blood off, it was all smiles. Hope someone got it on camera.'

'You're not *really* helping here,' I smiled weakly.

'We should stick it up on YouTube. Send it viral.' He stopped to gasp mock-theatrically. 'We could release it in 3D!'

I shot him a series of daggers that bounced harmlessly off his conk and we plodded on in silence until . . .

'So what's next, then?' he asked.

'What do you mean?'

'Well, you've broken theatre as we know it. What are you going to ruin . . . I mean, revolutionize next?'

It was becoming harder to work out why I was walking with him. Being on my own would have been better than this.

'I don't arse everything up, you know.'

'Hmm.'

'I don't!'

'Example?'

'Football!' I blurted out before I could think. 'What about the match I played? I was the only kid in school history to score a hat-trick on debut.'

'That *is* true,' he nodded. 'Shame none of them were at the right end, wasn't it?'

My skin crawled at the memory of the goals going in my own net, the pain in my head as the last one ricocheted in off my ear.

'Didn't they stretcher you off after the third?'

I nodded.

'Perforated ear drum, wasn't it?'

Another nod, and a blush to go with it.

I saw Sinus stifle a laugh as he spoke. 'Probably for the best though – got you off the pitch before your own team mates ripped you limb from limb.'

'Yeah, cheers, Sinus. I'd like to see you try and head the ball without bursting it.'

'I wouldn't even try,' he shrugged. 'Why do I need to make an idiot of myself when you do it well enough for us both?'

My head raced back to other humiliations: nearly setting fire to the science lab with a single piece of magnesium ribbon; nearly losing a finger to the bluntest of compasses; how I managed to give the whole class food poisoning after sampling my simple jam sponge. I mean, how unlucky could I be?

Sinus knew the answer.

'You must be cursed. I reckon it has to be something like that, and unless you break the spell you'll be like this all your life.'

I stared at him, wide-eyed. 'Wow. Thanks for the summary, pal. You've restored my confidence in a single sentence.'

'No problem. You're a friend. You'd do the same for me, I'm sure.'

I thought hard about how I could ridicule him, about stuff other than his ridiculous, showing-up-from-outer-space nose. Such as the fact that his trousers were always five centimetres too short for his legs, or that he always had enough wax in his ears to fuel a power cut in the dead of winter.

Or I could simply go for his other weakness. The fact that he was just so . . . vacant.

You see it wasn't *just* the nose that bought him the outsider tag. That alone would've seen the ridiculing stop by year seven, allowing him to slip into being one of the anonymous freaks who simply didn't exist to the others in our year.

The reason he still took such a kicking was that he was just so goddamn weird, in particular when it came to his wall fetish.

I don't know what it was about bricks and mortar, but it clearly fascinated him. He'd stand there smiling at any wall bigger than three square metres, head cocked at an angle, eyes boring into it, like he could knock it down with the power of his mind alone. He knew not to stand too close and stare though – he'd done it once, only to be shoved face first into the brickwork, his nose left so battered and bruised it looked like the last piece of meat left on the supermarket shelf.

I thought hard about reminding him about this, or any of his other weirdnesses, as he got stuck into me now, but I couldn't bring myself to do it.

What was the point? Insults bounced off him. Instead we walked in silence to Sinus's front wall, where he stopped and stared at it for a while.

'So I'll see you tomorrow, then?' I asked.

'Yup,' he answered, without looking up.

'Walk to school?'

'Yup.' His eyes didn't move from the bricks.

'I'll meet you here, then. Usual time.'

'I'll be here.'

'Sure you will,' I mumbled as I walked off, leaving him standing, trance-like.

I'd managed twenty metres before realizing I should tell him to keep tonight's debacle to himself.

As I turned, he was still staring at the wall.

'Probably best not to mention to my mum what happened,' I shouted. 'You know, with the play. You know how she gets.'

He nodded, although he wasn't watching me, and, besides, he knew the score with my mum. One loose word from him and I wouldn't be let out of the house this side of Christmas.

4

The day after Shakespeare's latest tragedy started much the same as any other, with me tumbling head first over the baby gate at the top of the stairs.

I swore loudly as my shoulder bounced off the first step, the bluest word I could mix on my pallet, followed by a kaleidoscope of filth for every other step, all fifteen of them.

By the time I reached the bottom, Mum had raced to meet me, face adopting the standard-issue panicky look she favoured this and every morning.

'What's up, Charlie?' She leaned in too close, features distorting.

'I fell down the stairs!' Talk about stating the obvious.

'Again? But how? I closed the gate to stop that happening!'

My insides crumbled at the thought of having this conversation again.

'No, Mum, I fell *because* of the gate. Why do you do this to me? I'm not a baby any more. I'm fourteen. Exclude the gate as a reason and you'll find I haven't fallen down the stairs in over ten years!'

'What nonsense,' she fussed as her hand scoured my head,

checking it for bumps. 'You went all the way down only last week.'

'BECAUSE THE GATE WAS SHUT!' I hollered. 'Take the gate away and I can manage them just fine. Please, Mum. Please. I don't need it there any more.'

She considered it for a nanosecond.

'I'll talk to your dad about it. See what we can do. Although we do have your *problem* to consider too, don't we?'

If there's one thing my mum loved, it was a problem. Especially if it meant she could smother me just that little bit harder. I feel Mum's arms around me a lot. Hugging, squeezing, stroking. Even when she's nowhere near me, I can still feel her arms, tight round my chest. Sometimes she makes it hard to breathe. I won't let her anywhere near me at school. The last thing I need is to be punished with the walk for being Mummy's brave little soldier.

The problem she was on about wasn't even a problem.

About eighteen months ago I'd had a fever. No big deal, just the flu and a temperature that made me a bit delirious in the middle of the night. She'd heard me stumbling down the stairs to the kitchen, found me sweating and swearing as I tried to stick my head inside the chest freezer. All right, so it wasn't my sanest moment, but I had a temperature of over a hundred – I wasn't playing with the fullest deck.

Three hours later and I was feeling fine apart from the embarrassment Mum heaped on top of me.

'You could have suffocated!' she'd yelped. 'What if you'd fallen in and the lid had come down on you? We'd never have known.'

'The freezer's full to the brim with an Ark's worth of meat, Mum. Noah couldn't squeeze a pair of woodlice in there, never mind me as well.'

'This is a big joke to you, isn't it? Well, I don't see anything funny in it at all, Charlie. Not a thing.'

So began a new wave of motherly paranoia like none before.

Every time I went to the toilet in the middle of the night, there she was. On the occasions I tried to pinch a late-night biscuit, I'd find her behind me, arms readied to perform the Heimlich in case of a Hobnob choking disaster.

I know, I know. It's not normal, but the problem was it was pointless arguing with her. The more I tried, the harder she dug her heels in.

When it came to me, she worried about *everything*, about whether *everything* was safe.

Take Christmas, for example. The happiest time of year, peace on earth and all that. A time for families doing things together, like decorating the tree.

Not in our house.

I was five years old before I was allowed to hang a bauble off a branch.

Christmas trees were dangerous, you see. Pine needles were sharp and all it took was one slip, one miscalculation and that was it – I could lose an eye.

I begged her so hard one year that she finally caved in, agreeing to let me help as long as I wore swimming goggles.

SWIMMING GOGGLES!

Can you imagine how I looked, goggled up in my own front room, with the nearest swimming pool over five miles away?

It took a bit of the magic away, I promise you.

In the end I sat and watched Dad do it: a rare moment when he wasn't frying rice in the kitchen. She never made *him* wear goggles, or even his specs. No, her paranoia only stretched as far as me, her only child.

I tried to ask Dad why she was so over-bearing, but I couldn't drag anything out of him either.

Better with a wok than he is with words, Mum always said about him, and I suppose she was right. It wasn't like he didn't understand. Him and Granddad had arrived in England from China when he was twelve, so he could speak English. He just chose not to, or to pretend not to understand. He could stay out of things that way. Out of Mum's war path, let her do the talking for them both.

'Can't you have a word with her?' I'd begged him.

He flashed me a look that said, *Really? Have you met her?*

'But if anyone can change her mind, it's you, Dad.'

'It's not that bad, is it?'

'Not that bad? She won't let me do anything. Or go anywhere.'

'Stop exaggerating.'

'Eh? Exaggerating? Dad, I wasn't allowed to go to a firework display until I was eleven because it was *perilous*. I had to twist her arm to even let me watch them through the double-glazing. I mean, what would she have said if I'd asked for a sparkler?'

'She's your mum.'

Man, I hated it when he said that. It was his stock answer. It said everything and nothing at the same time. It was the equivalent of *Shut up and get on with it. Nothing's going to change.*

'And that's it, is it? That's the gem of wisdom you can offer me?'

He shrugged sadly and patted me on my arm, his hands rough and calloused from years spent holding a steaming hot wok.

'I've stuff to chop,' he added, pointing to the safety of his kitchen.

'Don't let me come between you and your sweet and sour balls,' I sighed and headed back up the stairs, kicking the stair gate as I reached the top.

It hurt.

I hated that chuffing gate.

5

So while we're on the subject of extreme physical pain, let me tell you about the walk of shame.

Every school has its own variation, whether it's having your head held down a flushing lav or being buried to the neck in an ant-infested long jump pit, but ours is just that bit special. In the true spirit of the digital age, it's got that special flash-mob feel to it.

I knew I'd be doing *the walk* after the play debacle. It was inevitable. I'd done it for far less in the past. What I didn't know was when.

There have been times when they've toyed with me, let a few days pass, enough to plant a seed of hope that maybe, for once, they'd forgotten. They never did, though. Once that shoot popped its head tentatively out of the ground, that was when they took the most delight in stamping on it, on me.

Mobile phones don't help. Nor does Facebook. Once a post goes up, notifying that a walk is taking place, it only takes minutes for word to get around. No one ever 'likes' the post or dares to comment; that would only give the teachers the evidence needed to step in and bust heads.

Instead, students simply clock the news and turn up in number, even if it's to watch rather than participate.

The walk isn't a complicated form of torture: you don't need a pair of pliers or an electricity socket nearby, in fact you don't even need a big number of bodies to inflict it. I've done the walk with only four people involved. Doesn't mean it hurts any less. The shorter the tunnel, the harder they tend to kick.

You know when the walk's upon you. And not just because of the people lining up: you can sense it, smell the anticipation. I've always imagined it's like in Roman times with the gladiators. Except then, the crowd were seeing a spectacle, a competition. If they wanted to lend me a whip or spear, then maybe we could make the comparison, but as it stands, forget it. *The walk* makes David versus Goliath look like a fair match-up.

Once the buzz hits you, you know what's coming. Bodies step forward from all sides, forming a corridor about double your width. Wide enough to walk down, narrow enough to be threatening. They pace inwards in unison, with almost military intent, adding to the menace.

And that's it – once the corridor is in place, all you have to do is walk down it. Simple enough until the legs start to fly and you're leaping like the hero in some crappy 1980s video game.

People will try to tell you that there are strategies for surviving the walk unscathed, but I can tell you, as its most experienced subject, that there aren't.

I've tried them all. Sprinting, jumping, hopping – I've even considered cartwheeling in a moment of sheer panic. All of them (bar the last one) sound fine in theory, but I can guarantee you that at some point a flailing leg is going to catch you. And once it does? Game over. Cover your vitals, stay on your feet and get through it the best you can. Oh, and never show them you're hurt. Weep on the inside only.

I've seen it ruin kids. Reduce heroes to puddles in the space of ten pairs of legs. But not me: they can kick as hard and as long as they want, but they'll not floor me. I won't give them the satisfaction. Instead I feed off it, store up every bit of energy they're wasting for my own means.

Because once I find that thing? That illusive thing that separates me from them, well, they'll know about it.

I'll be so superior to them that I won't need to kick down in their direction. I'll be flying so high, I'd never be able to reach. And more importantly, they won't reach me.

6

'Special Fried Nice?' I sighed into the phone, trying to sound friendly, even though the phrase made me want to hack out my own tongue with a splintered chopstick.

It's bad enough fulfilling every racial stereotype possible by being a Chinese kid who lives above a takeaway, without the takeaway having the lamest name known to man.

I had no idea what was wrong with The Blue Lotus, as it was when Dad bought it, but Mum had been insistent, reckoned we had to stamp our own identity on the place. She said that the old owners had been a laughing stock, known for everything being battered within an inch of its life, regardless of whether it was edible or not.

So when she saw a hairdressers off Newland Ave called Curl Up And Dye, she reckoned we should copy their idea, find a clever play on words, something people would remember every time they felt hungry.

Special Fried Nice was the final choice. It was a toss up between that and Wokever You Want. Both sounded lame to me, but hey, I was just their goggle-wearing, firework-starved, delivery-boy of a son. What did I know?

It was all right for Mum. She wasn't the one picking up

the phone every night, listening to the sniggers as I took the orders, wondering if the dodgy name was enough to see me doing *the walk* by nine a.m. the next day. I never ruled it out.

Mum spent as little time in the takeaway as possible. It's not like she thought it was beneath her, it was just too chaotic, a health and safety nightmare that she couldn't bear to stand by and watch.

Instead, for as long as I could remember, her focus in life had been night school and a multitude of new, exciting and frankly often bizarre courses.

Mum was addicted to further education, you see. It almost didn't matter what the course was, she'd give it a whirl.

Flower arranging
Basket weaving
Pottery
Carpentry
Bricklaying
Origami

There was no topic too macho or girly, no subject too laborious for her to try. She'd done them all, but the weirdest thing was she had nothing to show for it, no certificates or diplomas, and even more weirdly, no examples of what she'd made. In all the years she'd been going, she had never once brought home so much as a papier mâché ashtray.

I found it strange, course I did. I wanted to find a way of asking her why without looking smug or sneery, but she was so passionate about each of her courses, never missing a single night of lessons, that I never did. It seemed cruel. Maybe she was just a bit crap at them, too embarrassed to bring anything home. And anyway, her being out three nights a week suited me. I could get away with more when Dad was on shift, even if the kitchen remained out of bounds. (All those knives and hot oil? Dad's life was barely worth living as it was, if she came home to find a scratch on me, he'd be in the next batch of frozen chow mein.)

Taking orders over the phone, armed with a TV that could pick up *only* the origami channel, had a shelf-life.

An hour a night was all I could take. Any period longer than that and I had folded everything in sight into a paper swan. Menus, newspapers, customers if they stood still long enough. It was at moments like that that I thanked the heavens for the one victory I'd scored over Mum in all her years of fussing.

It was a small triumph, but one I celebrated wildly. It was my equivalent of winning the Champions League and Nobel Peace Prize combined.

Two years ago, after months of nagging, pleading and spectacular crocodile-tearing, I'd finally convinced her to let me make home deliveries for Special Fried Nice. And even better than that, I'd persuaded her to buy me a vehicle to make them on.

This was monumental news. Bikes had been off limits for years after I'd fallen off mine aged six, taking a centimetre of skin off my knee in the process.

After a lengthy spell waiting in A&E, where the doctors first laughed, then shouted when she refused to leave without an X-ray, the bike had been stashed in the shed behind a dozen broken deep-fat fryers, never to be ridden again.

As a result, the day when my new bike arrived should've been better than any Christmas Day EVER.

In the history of humankind.

Unfortunately, it became the sort of day you want to erase from your head with a breezeblock.

Instead of a gleaming, sleek mountain bike, with lightweight aluminium frame and Shimano gears, I was faced with a 1970s lead-framed TRIKE, complete with basket and littered with more lights than an airport runway.

Mum mistook my tears for happiness, pulling me into her as I shook with the pain of the humiliation ahead.

As if that wasn't enough, she pulled the bonus presents out too. A wide array of fluorescent clothing that had been reclaimed from a sixteen-stone lollipop man, and a horse-riding helmet with a torch gaffer-taped to the top of it.

I died inside.

She beamed with pride as I stood before her like the most luminous, ridiculous star in the sky.

'Now, there are rules to this delivery business. You only deliver in the hours of daylight. Any orders taken after seven p.m. will be handled by someone else.'

'But it doesn't get dark until nine!'

'It's seven or nothing.'

'But I've got all these lights.'

'And you'll use them all, and your safety gear, on *every* delivery you make.'

'Eh?'

'EVERY delivery, Charlie.'

'But I'll blind every motorist in town,' I pleaded. 'People will stop and stare. They'll ridicule me. They'll take photos thinking I'm a low-flying UFO.'

'You'll be safe. That's my only concern and my final word.'

I shot Dad a pleading look that he deflected with his standard *She's your mum* look. I made a note to think up some kind of revenge, then grimaced as the riding helmet was wedged on to my skull.

'Well, go on then. Give it a whirl.'

'Maybe later, Mum. It'll be dark in four hours. Maybe I shouldn't risk it.'

'A quick go will be fine, I'm sure.' Her face, though, said otherwise.

I pulled my leg over the crossbar, placed my feet on the pedals and pushed.

Nothing.

I tried again, and again, but nothing moved. It wasn't until I stood on the pedals and strained like a herniated hippo that the cogs finally gave and I shunted forward, the three wheels turning a whole revolution before stopping again.

A gaggle of small children on the other side of the road had laughed and pointed. It felt like the first step towards the ultimate embarrassment and it was courtesy of my own flesh and blood.

Turns out I was right too. And wrong at the same time. As the Trike of Doom did eventually, after two years of mental and physical pain, actually lead me down a road other than Humiliation Street.

It was an exciting road. Different to the cul-de-sacs I was usually wheeled down. This road was exciting and unexpected. A super-highway with only one signpost, which read simply 'Popularity, this way'.

There aren't many brilliant things about the town where I live, but every time I get on the trike to deliver pork balls to the obese guy at 59 Bellfield Drive, I thank every lucky star there is for the flat surface in front of me.

I'd adjusted to the trike after a few painful, cramp-inducing months, but it was never going to be a speedy ride. My thigh muscles might now be as muscly as Popeye's arms, but it didn't make a difference – the steel rhino (as I'd named it) refused to ever move quicker than a crawl.

It had been especially mortifying in the early days. Five-year-olds with stabilizers on their bikes would speed past me, laughing as they went. A bird even landed on my handlebars one day, thinking I was a branch waving gently in the coastal breeze. At one point it was considering building a nest and moving its family in.

It was the biggest nightmare ever, and time, no matter what they tell you, is a lousy healer.

Here I was, a pimped-up luminous bogey heaving my way along Carr Lane, the *SPEEDY Special Fried Nice* sign on my basket, reminding everyone that it was me, the idiot Charlie Han on board.

I was too busy dealing with the humiliation to realize that everything was about to change ...

It was my final delivery of the day (even though the sun was still burning the back of my neck) and I heard a trundling behind me, growing ever louder.

I braced myself, expecting the usual harassment from a gang of savage CBeebies fans, when a lad about my age shot past on a skateboard. And man, he was travelling.

I felt his wake swish past me, and maybe it was the fact that he neither noticed nor abused me, but it was without doubt the coolest thing I had ever seen. It was like he was floating as he weaved along the road.

Instantly, I forgot all about the delicacies in my basket, stood on my pedals and fought with all my might; I had to keep him in sight, see exactly what he was up to. Fortunately he stopped by a bench fifty metres on.

I pedalled closer, trying to look cool despite sweating furiously. He still wasn't the slightest bit interested in me, and he hadn't stopped to *rest* on the bench. Instead he was skating at it, full pelt.

It was terrifying, the sort of clumsy, idiotic thing *I* normally did, and for a second I thought I'd discovered a long-lost brother. It was excruciating to watch, but I couldn't help myself. Here I was, seeing myself through other people's eyes ...

But then something strange happened. Strange and wonderful and utterly, utterly cool.

Just as the kid reached the bench, just as he was about to hospitalize himself, he jumped.

And you know what? The board jumped with him. It stuck to his feet like glue, sliding him and it effortlessly along the seat, sliding, sliding, sliding until . . . whack! The wheels landed back on the pavement – and on he skated.

I did two things when that happened. First, I picked my jaw up off the floor, and second, I clapped. Like a loon. Even though he didn't hear me, even though I was being watched suspiciously by an elderly couple on the other side of the road.

I saw the old man make a spiralling motion to his temple with a finger, but I didn't care. I'd just seen the greatest thing EVER. And I *had* to see more.

Looking up, I saw the kid turn left on to Well Lane and guessed where he was going: the park.

With new energy I screamed forward at half a mile an hour, not daring to stop until the kid on the flying board came back into view.

It didn't take me long to find him and twenty others.

They were grouped by the old disused paddling pool. Some of them skating, others sitting on their boards talking excitedly to each other.

The paddling pool had been empty for years. Parents stopped using it when a kid contracted some weird disease that hadn't been seen since the seventeenth century. It had sat sad and drained until the BMX-ers found it, and eventually, alongside the riders, came the skaters.

There was something new slap in the middle of it now, though. A wooden ramp, U-shaped and towering. It was so huge I couldn't believe I hadn't noticed it before. Had it been made of brick, Sinus would have stared at it for a month.

It loomed above the skaters, three times their height, with a ledge at each end wide enough for them to stand and gently brick themselves at the drop.

I left the rhino grazing beside a tree, unlocked (hoping someone would be mad enough to nick it), before sitting cross-legged a short distance from the pool.

It. Was. Amazing.

One after another they launched themselves off the ledge, hurtling to the bottom at breakneck speed before whipping skywards again. And when they reached the top they flew, the wheels spinning under their feet, backs arched as they grabbed the board and twisted, just in time for the wheels to hit the floor again.

My mouth was set in a 'WOW' shape for fifteen minutes, utterly, utterly transfixed.

And do you know what the best thing was?

Sometimes, quite a few times even, they fell off their boards. And when they did, they looked awkward and daft. But no one laughed at them. They'd help each other up, with a slap on their back and a high five before trying again.

That's when I knew this was my chance. I'd found something where it didn't matter if I was a bit clumsy. That was part of it. I could feel the pats on my spine already, my heart racing, excitement building. THIS WAS IT!

Until my phone rang and Dad whispered into my ear.

'Have you had a puncture, son? Number 59 are screaming for their food.'

I felt my dream deflate quicker than a tyre.

There I was, dreaming of skateboarding notoriety, and all I had was a steel rhino. It couldn't have been any more useless, and I knew I had to do something about it.

But how could I afford my own board? And more importantly, how could I ever get this new, dangerous love past Mum?

8

Sinus didn't break his gaze from the brickwork to answer my question. He was stood so close to the wall, all it would take was one sneeze to decorate the whole thing.

'Skateboarding? Don't know much about it. But tell me if you do take it up, cos I'll need to save up for a funeral suit.'

'Don't be soft,' I laughed. 'It's not that dangerous. And anyway, I've watched them down at the half-pipe. It's no big deal if they fall off. It's all part of it.'

Two eyes flicked my way, joined by a pair of raised eyebrows. The head shook with pity, then refocused.

Maybe Sinus wasn't the right person to talk to, but I didn't really have any other options. There was no way I was going to ask Mum for cash for a board, and Dad was so under her thumb that he'd probably blab if I asked him. So that left me with Sinus.

I'd thought of nothing else since my first trip to the ramp a week ago. Had Googled every page on skating that existed, and the more I saw, the more obsessed I became. I'd found footage of this guy, Tony Hawk, who they said was the daddy of all skaters, and he did things that defied logic or gravity. I looked hard for the wires that held him up, or signs of CGI tomfoolery, but there were none. The guy was legend.

I devoured every clip, every interview there was and they all told me the same thing. That I was destined to do this, that this would be the *thing* that lifted me out of the gutter.

Affording the board, though, was a real problem. New ones were way out of my league, especially as my money-box contained £1.14 in coppers, a half-penny from 1975 and a Justin Bieber badge. Don't ask me how *that* got there. I hadn't a clue, but suspected foul play of the Sinus kind.

Tips from the deliveries hadn't exactly flowed into my pockets either. The rhino was so slow that food was lukewarm when it arrived on people's doorsteps, and Dad spent more time taking complaints than people's orders.

I'd tried eBay too, bidding on anything that came up within a ten-mile radius, but every time I thought I'd picked up a stupid £1 bargain, someone would gazump me and my dream deck would disappear for the princely sum of £1.14, a penny farthing and two Bieber badges.

I was failing. Failing before I had even begun.

And that's why I'd turned to Sinus. Talk about last resorts.

'So what I really need to find is someone with a spare board,' I sighed.

'Sounds like it.' He wasn't interested and wasn't hiding the fact. Instead he was now busy sticking his nose deep inside a new-looking notebook.

'Either that or find someone who tried it then gave up. Someone who'd give me the board cos they didn't want it,' I persevered.

'Yeah, cos that'll happen. Keep dreaming, sunshine.'

And that was it. That was the sum total of Sinus's input.

We sat there for twenty minutes, him alternating between scribbling furiously and staring dreamily at the science lab wall in front of us.

I'd just about given up when he finally spoke.

'Of course, you could just ask Bunion if you can have his.'

I stared at him. Bunion. His big brother, with feet so big that they made Sinus's nose look like a pimple.

I often wondered what was going on with the genes in his family. I was relieved Sinus's parents had only had two kids. A boy with ears that dragged along the floor wouldn't have stood a chance in life.

'You're kidding me?' I yelled at him. 'Bunion's got one? Bunion's had one all this time and you didn't think to tell me?'

'You only mentioned it twenty minutes ago.'

'And that's how long it takes sound to bypass your nose and reach your brain, is it?'

He batted the insult away as ever. 'You listen through your ears, not your nose, numbnut.'

I hated it when my insults fell flat, especially as his never did.

Irritated, I stood and walked away with purpose. Sinus breathed heavily as he scampered to catch up.

'Where are you going?' he asked, not wanting to miss the next gripping instalment of *Charlie Has a Deathwish*.

'Where do you think?' I muttered. 'To see your Bunion.'

9

You had to look hard to find something positive about Bunion Sedgley's appearance.

He was no pin-up. In fact, it looked like he'd been tortured with the biggest ugly stick known to man.

The only positive I'd ever found to his unique look was that he'd never get knocked over by any kind of wind, gale, hurricane or tropical typhoon. His feet were way too long to ever let that happen. They were the human equivalent of tree roots.

Shoes had been specially made for him since he was seven years old; you could've strapped a couple of kayaks to his feet and he still wouldn't be able to wiggle his big toes comfortably.

He was no good at things like football, obviously. Each boot would've needed a hundred and fifty studs to grip the turf, but, weirdly, I could never remember him ever doing *the walk* at school. Didn't want to be on the end of it if he was doing the kicking either. He'd boot your leg clean off.

He was also just like Sinus. If his physical freakishness bothered him, it never showed. In fact, there was a real arrogance about him.

He had a habit of rocking back and forth on the balls of his feet, swaying with such range that I always felt seasick after two minutes in his company. He knew this and used it like a weapon, especially once he knew I was after something.

'Course you can have the board . . .' he grinned slimily.

I didn't buy into his kindness and wondered what might be wrong with the deck. Was it actually fifteen metres long to accommodate his delicate pinkies?

'. . . but it'll cost you.'

'I've already told you, Bunion, I haven't got any cash, mate.'

He gasped theatrically. 'I'm not talking about money. What do you think I am? An animal?'

He circled me with a single step. 'No, what I'm talking about is rent. Every week you have the board, you can pay me in food from your dad's place. I've always been very partial to his prawn chow mein. Four times a week should cover it.'

'Four times a week? Do you know how much prawns cost?'

'Well, they're hardly king-sized, are they? The ones your dad serves up are more like shrimps.'

'Once a week.'

'Three times,' he insisted.

'Twice, and I'll throw in prawn crackers.'

'And a pickled egg!' He was salivating now.

'Deal,' I groaned.

'Been a pleasure,' he beamed, and strode off to the shed,

returning twenty minutes later with a skateboard-shaped cobweb.

'Here you go.' He forced it into my hands like it were cow dung. 'Never liked it anyway. Mug's game.'

'Thanks,' I added, though I didn't mean it. What on earth was I going to do with this? It was in worse shape than the steel rhino.

'I'll expect first payment on Thursday, six thirty. Don't be late.'

'Whatever,' I mumbled, and made a pledge to litter his food with seasoning sourced from each of my ears.

My bad mood didn't last long, though. Once I'd sneaked the board in past Mum and chiselled away at the years of cobwebs and dust, it didn't look too bad. It wasn't a four-wheeled equivalent of the trike anyway.

It was plain black on the top, with a ghoulish devil laughing inanely underneath. There wasn't a scratch on the design, more evidence of its criminal lack of use.

The only problem were the wheels. They were luminous red, exactly what I needed to stand out when whipping up and down the half-pipe, but they were so rusted and under-used that they wouldn't turn.

I spent half an hour with my fists wrapped around them, persuading them to give, but even after adding half a tin of WD-40, they still wouldn't move.

In a last-gasp effort, I nicked a bottle of Dad's homemade cooking oil from the kitchen and splashed it on each wheel. I left it for two minutes, hoping, begging, for it to work, and you know what? After a couple of creaky spins they started to turn, faster and faster until I could hear the oil heating up so much I could've stir-fried veg in it.

I punched the air in celebration. This was it. It had to be the start of something.

I was so full of confidence that I planted my feet on the deck, pushing my back heel on to the tail of it to flick it skywards like the other lads did.

The board shot from under me and crashed into my wardrobe, chipping a huge shard of wood away in the process. I fell backwards and landed heavily, my head whacking against the bed leg. Throb didn't even come close.

I groaned loudly but had no time for self-pity as Mum's footsteps thundered up the stairs.

'Charlie? Charlie, love? Are you all right?'

Without hesitation I leapt to my feet and dived for the board, ramming it under the bed just as she appeared in the room. I must have looked like a proper tool, hanging out from under the bed, a bruise like a tennis ball swelling on my head.

'Have you hurt yourself?' she cried.

'No, no. I'm fine, honest.'

'Are you sure?'

'Completely.' Although my skull was screaming otherwise.

She eyed the room suspiciously, looking for whatever had mugged me. Her eyes fell on Dad's oil.

'What on earth are you doing up here?' she asked, picking the bottle up.

My head spun, causing my mouth to spit out the most ridiculous line ever.

'Dry skin,' I gabbled. 'On my elbow. Just trying to stop it itching.'

'Well, don't use *this*.'

And so began a rigorous examination of my elbows, knees and every other joint on my body. Only when she found no evidence of warts, ringworm, eczema, psoriasis or rickets did she finally leave the room, promising to check up on me in twenty minutes.

Once her steps had faded on the stairs, I dared to retrieve the board from under the bed, wincing at the first scratch to ever grace its surface. It could've been way worse.

This was going to be harder than I thought. It wasn't like Mum afforded me any kind of privacy in life. Secrets weren't really an option. And even if they were, would I ever be able to stand upright on the blooming thing, never mind ride it?

So began the training. The gruelling, arse-numbing, top-secret training. The kind of training usually reserved for SAS recruits and clandestine wings of the FBI. Or that's how I saw it anyway. Thinking of it that way dulled the pain that my body was in almost hourly.

I lost count of the number of bruises hidden beneath my clothes. I had so many that you couldn't count them; they merged into each other in one big aching mess. My body was the equivalent of David Beckham's tattooed arms – well, apart from that girls would've screamed at me for a very different reason.

Obviously.

It was difficult keeping them out of Mum's sight (the bruises, not the girls), especially when I was changing for bed or getting ready for a bath. She had an annoying habit (one of many) of appearing at these times, asking if I wanted bubbles adding to the water, or whether I needed a drink beside my bed.

I mean, LEAVE IT OUT, MUM!

Not that I said that to her, of course; instead I took more care to lock the bathroom door behind me, jamming anything I could find against it, even spare bog rolls, for that extra, double-quilted security.

Sometimes I felt guilty that she annoyed me so much. I mean she was my mum, and I could see in her eyes that she really *was* worried and wanted the best for me. Most of the time, though, I couldn't deal with it and sulkily toed the line like Dad, feeling more and more depressed. I began to understand why he said so little in life.

But as painful as it was, both in my head and for my body, I refused to give up on the skating. In the rare moments that I managed to stay upright, it was the most exciting feeling . . . even if I wasn't moving.

I spent hours at first just standing on it, allowing myself to lean further and further to the side without falling, feeling the wheels threaten to turn under me. I imagined myself at the ramp, the board thundering beneath as we soared skywards, hearing the gasping of the wind and other skaters as we pulled off a trick never before seen on British shores.

All right, this was a way off – I hadn't really mastered moving on it yet, never mind flying – but the dream of it excited me, inspired me, pushed me onward.

Once I was upright and steady, I risked trying to move, staying behind at school once the yard had emptied, rolling slowly across the car park where the tarmac was smoothest.

It was difficult to practise without being seen, or without upsetting Sinus, who couldn't understand why he now had to walk home on his own every day.

'Oh,' he'd huff. 'Better things to do, eh?'

I didn't want to upset him, and practising at school was far from ideal. I'd had to dive into the bushes in the name of secrecy on more occasions than my body cared to remember. Still, another bruise was better than being seen before I was ready, which, by my rate of progress, would be the year 2037.

My problem was simple. I just couldn't balance once I was moving. No matter how hard I tried. Crouching didn't work and neither did sticking my backside out. How could the others make it look so easy when I was flailing like Bambi on the frickin' ice?

The breakthrough came just as I was about to give up. I was delivering on the rhino, feeling properly grumpy, when I hit a broken bottle in the road. The tyres flattened in a second, leaving me stranded with two bags of takeaway for a couple of notorious moaners. The guy at number 59 had threatened to make me wear his food the last time I was late, and as teriyaki trousers weren't exactly on trend this summer . . . ? Well, you get the picture.

I was panicking. The only option I had was the board, stashed in the basket. I'd been trying to practise *between* deliveries, but now? Well, it had to be worth a go. So, with a bag of food in each hand, I rested my left foot on the board and pushed with the right.

Quite where the bravery or belief came from I'm not sure, but after a shuddery start I was moving. Moving without falling. Moving without bruising another inch of my body.

It was amazing. All right, I wasn't setting a land speed record or anything, but I was upright. Upright and moving! And do you know what made the difference? The bags of food. They acted like stabilizers on a bike, keeping me balanced and on track.

I can't even begin to describe the happiness in my gut,

but I knew it was growing, seeping through every vein in my body. So this was how adrenalin felt. Mum had kept me away from it for so long, as long as I could remember, that I wished I could shout her now to tell her, show her, that she was wrong to be so worried. No one died; I could do this and be safe at the same time.

The journey to number 59 was impossible to describe. There was the odd wobble, of course, but I'll never forget the feeling as I overtook a seven-year-old on his micro-scooter. I had to stop myself from turning round and striking a pose.

The fat gut at the first delivery looked shocked when I pitched up on his doorstep.

He checked his watch, then checked again, grabbing the bag to find his food hot for once.

'Stroll on,' he grinned. 'No need for a microwave tonight,' and shoved a tenner into my hand. 'Keep the change.'

£1.50 tip! Result. The closest I'd ever got to a tip before, after holding my hand out expectantly, was him telling me never to wipe my arse with a broken bottle. I knew instantly I'd put the cash towards new parts for the board.

With only one bag of food, though, the rest of the journey was wobbly at best.

I had to scoop the contents of the carton back in after one particularly eggy fall, but I still managed to roll along, throwing my arms out to the side if I felt like I was going to come off.

I grinned stupidly at the second guy's house as he eyed his bag suspiciously. It looked like a bomb had gone off in it. I didn't care about the lack of a tip, because I'd done it.

I was Charlie Han. Skateboarding prospect. And I couldn't wait to step foot on that ramp.

Secrets are for other people, not me.

It's not how I'd choose it, but there it is.

I'd like to be able to take one and bury it deep inside me, revelling in how smug it made me feel. Other people manage it, why not me?

But instead they burn a hole inside my brain, until I can feel their heat seeping outwards towards my skin, till my face is beaming like a beacon. Anyone within a two-mile radius can see what's going on within seconds.

Especially Mum.

She leaned over the breakfast table, her hand shooting to my forehead, where it rested.

'I'm not sure you should be going to school today, young man.' She looked worried. As usual.

I continued to chew on my Cheerios, playing down her concern.

'You're hot . . .' She sighed. 'Are you sure you're feeling OK? Any rashes, or other symptoms?'

'I'm fine, Mum. Really.'

'But you're sweating.'

'It's nothing. I've been working out in my room, that's

all. Press-ups and that.' I flexed my biceps but felt unimpressed. There was more meat on a butcher's pencil.

'Well, you look peaky to me. Perhaps you should stay at home today. No point taking risks.'

I leapt from the chair, banging my head on the lampshade above.

'There's no need!' I yelled, more urgently than I should have. 'Honestly. Stop fussing. There's nothing wrong with me.'

Staying at home wasn't an option. Today was the day I'd plucked up the courage to get down the skate park for the first time. The day when the kids at school would start to see me differently, or for the first time see me at all.

The last two months had all led to this point. The hours of practice, the endless books and articles I'd devoured. I was ready. It had to be today, or else I'd always find an excuse. And I couldn't live with that.

'Please, Mum.' I lowered my voice, seeing the hurt on her face. 'There's no need to worry. I feel fine. Better than fine. Magic, in fact. But I'll put another layer on if it makes you feel better.'

'You're a good lad, and I'm sorry to fuss.' She looked all misty. 'First sign of a cold, though, and I want you home, got me?'

'Got you,' and to hide my guilt I gave her a hug, trying not to grimace when she squeezed my bruises that bit too hard.

'OK, Mum, you can let go now.'

She didn't. I practically had to slither to the floor to escape. I'm sure as I reached the door I heard a loud sniffle from her direction. I hoped it was due to a cold, not anything I'd said.

Five minutes later, though, I was doing a brilliant impression of Mum at her eccentric best.

There I was, backside in the air, rifling on all fours under the bush at the end of the road, branches and leaves flying everywhere until I'd unearthed my board.

I'd been hiding it there for the past few weeks, since Mum had almost found it 'tidying' my room.

She did that from time to time, although we both knew she wasn't really interested in making it look neater.

What she was really doing was looking for anything dangerous in there, a sharp-cornered exercise book or a dodgy zip on my jeans that could injure me grievously.

She always left empty-handed, of course, without the death-inducing ninja throwing stars or grade-three plutonium that I'd stashed on top of my wardrobe for a rainy day.

Hiding the board outside was a risk, I knew, and my heart always thudded in my chest until I found it again, but it was the best option I had.

I'd spent quite a bit on it now, paid for by the tips I'd zoomed around town to collect, and as a result it didn't feel like Bunion's board any more. It was mine. Tailor-made to my own spec. I liked to think no one could skate on it but me.

As my fingers rested on its wheels, my heart rate fell in relief, only to jump skywards again when a hand gripped me from behind.

I turned, head spinning, fearing a rocket from Mum, only to find Sinus towering over me, his nose, as always, right in the middle of my business.

'What are you doing, soft lad?'

I grabbed his jumper in relief, not sure whether to kiss him or whack him for sneaking up.

'Nothing,' I yelled, stashing the board into my bag as best I could.

'That a skateboard?'

I stared at him, mystified by the sheer idiocy of his statement, wondering if it was actually some kind of trick question.

'Er, yep?'

'You still doing that then, are you?' There was a hint of hurt on his face.

You see, the thing was, the skating had kind of taken Sinus's place. I really didn't think it would bother him, had always imagined I would be replaced in his life by a new, impressive-looking wall. But from the narked expression on his face, I'd clearly got that wrong.

'And how's it going? Lost many teeth yet?'

I showed him my pearly whites. 'Not a single problem,' I lied, not mentioning my body's worth of bruises.

'Can't say the same for our Bunion,' he huffed. 'He's put on a stone in weight since you started dealing to him. Mum wants to put him on a diet. Keeps threatening him with one of them fat camps if he doesn't stop eating prawn crackers.'

The whole slavery deal with Bunion hadn't done much for my stress levels either. I'd had to invent orders to Dad, then come back without money for them, claiming the punter had refused to pay. Made me realize how lucky I was that Dad was so quiet. Anyone with a temper would've been banging on doors waving a cleaver until they coughed up!

As a result I felt nothing for the fat boy Bunion. Served the greedy git right. He could've lent me the board without payment if he'd really wanted.

We started plodding towards school, Sinus flicking through his notebook as we walked. I had no idea what he'd written in there, but he looked properly pleased with himself.

'So how good are you, then?' he asked.

'What, at skating?'

'No, ballet. Of course skating.'

'I can get by.'

'You doing tricks and that?'

'Not really. Not dared yet. But I can turn now.'

'You can TURN? Sweet lord!' His words dripped with sarcasm. 'Must make the last few weeks seem SO worthwhile.'

He was getting on my last nerve. Did he have to pick holes in every single thing I did? It wasn't as if he was filling his life with anything better. What was *he* doing to stop others thinking he was a freak? At least I was trying.

'You know, you could try supporting me instead of laughing. I heard on the grapevine that that's what friends do these days.'

He looked at me, completely baffled.

'Eh?'

'Why *do* you hang around with me, Sinus? Seriously. Do you even like me?'

'That's got absolutely nothing to do with anything, Charlie,' he said, deadly serious. 'Don't you get it? We fit, don't we? No one else wants to be mates with us, so we might as well just get on with it.'

He meant it, but I tried not to believe it or let my newfound confidence crumble as a result. Instead I shook my head and marched on.

'What?' he asked. 'What did I say?'

'Nothing. You haven't said anything. Nothing that I shouldn't have expected anyway.'

'Don't be like that,' he moaned through his nose. 'Tell you what. I'll come watch you. On your board. Tonight after school.'

'Wow, that's really big of you,' I said sarcastically.

His chest filled with pride as he slapped me on my back. His irony radar was well out of kilter.

'That's just how I roll,' he grinned. 'That's what friends do!'

There was no answer to that. Instead I walked on, not stopping when he became distracted by a newly plastered wall at the school gates.

This was a bad idea. Terrible, in fact. The worst idea since the captain of the *Titanic* forgot to wear his specs on that final night shift.

I swear the ramp had grown another metre overnight. Either that or I'd shrunk.

I didn't know which possibility was worse.

Sinus wasn't making things any easier either. Not that that should have come as a surprise.

'Ha!' he shrieked. 'You are kidding me? Are you seriously going to throw yourself off that thing?'

'I wasn't planning to,' I sighed, 'but I might chuck *you* off it if you don't shut up.'

'You can try.' He shoulder-bumped me, a little harder than a friend really should, causing me to drop my board with a right old clatter.

I picked it up sheepishly, hoping the kids by the ramp hadn't noticed.

'I think I'll stick to the other bits of the park for now. You know, just to ease myself in.' I was talking to myself really, but of course Sinus heard.

'Good thinking. Why don't you have a paddle in the

shallow end? Get your trunks on and I'll grab the hose.' He snorted through his nose, dislodging a bogey the size of a family car. *Classy*.

'Do us a favour and sit here, will you?' I motioned to the grass outside the skate area. 'I think your support might overpower me otherwise.'

'Good idea.' He threw himself down and became immediately fixated on both toilet wall *and* his notebook. With a bit of luck he'd be staring at them for the next hour and not me.

My heart was thumping out of my chest as I walked through the gate; it felt like I had the chance to forget a lifetime's embarrassments and start again. Properly.

Immediately, I knocked a kid off his deck as he sailed past.

'Sorry!' I yelled.

He waved back with a grin as he climbed back on board. My heart clambered back down inside my chest, warning me not to cock up again.

There were bodies everywhere. All of them flying in different directions: some of them higher in the air than I thought humanly possible. You could feel the wind whistle as they went past; it was every bit as exciting as I thought it would be.

I settled on the edge of a bench, only for another skater to use it as a ramp. He didn't bother telling me to move first. He was so in control that he cut the air beside me, missing intentionally by centimetres. In that moment I fell in love even more.

Two lads were watching, filming the move on their phones, whooping encouragement before sliding towards me. I knew them from school, year ten kids. All floppy fringes and awkward shuffling feet. It seemed impossible to imagine them being graceful on a board.

'We know you, don't we?' the taller one asked.

'Yeah, you're the kid from the Chinese chippy. The special-needs one.'

I didn't dare correct him. Anything I could come up with under that kind of pressure would only reinforce his opinion, especially with my squeak of a voice.

The taller lad, who was sporting a flimsy, misguided attempt at a beard, pointed and smiled.

'Yeah, I know you. You're the one who broke the caretaker's leg. Legendary fall that one. BIG ladder!'

'Fifteen pins he had put in,' the other one chirped.

This wasn't quite the level of anonymity I'd hoped for.

'Charlie,' I gabbled, offering my hand.

'Dan,' said one.

'Stan,' said the other, and they both grabbed my hand in an elaborate shake that I struggled to keep up with. They were more dexterous than they were intelligent. I wondered if I should make it easier for them by changing my name to rhyme with theirs.

'So how long have you been skating?' asked Stan, eyeing my deck.

'Not long. Few weeks.' I didn't want to say any longer in case I stunk. I wanted them to be impressed, not appalled.

'Cracking deck. New wheels, eh?'

I looked at them, hoping I'd made a good choice.

'Yeah, been saving up my wages. Wanted something that gave me the edge.'

I really hoped they hadn't seen me on the steel rhino. I didn't think I could ever live that down.

'Belters, they are. Not cheap neither.' They spun the wheels quickly, practically salivating at the speed.

My board opened up a whole line of conversation, and even though they were older than me, and obviously way better skaters, they were kind of, well, *interested*. In *me*. They asked where I'd been practising and, more importantly, what tricks I'd mastered.

'Not many,' I blushed. 'Been concentrating on not falling off really.'

CRINGE! Wrong thing to say? I had no idea but feared the worst.

Dan waved his hand dismissively. 'Nah, you don't want to worry about wiping out. Folk who stay on their feet obviously aren't pushing hard enough.'

'True,' agreed Stan. 'Check this bad boy out.' And he rolled up his sleeve to reveal a bruise that matched any of mine. 'Did this on the library steps,' he beamed proudly. 'Managed the first six. Seventh one legged me up, though.'

'You'll nail it next time, bruv,' Dan said, slapping his mate roughly on the back.

'Too right,' I added, wondering where I should whack him too, or whether that would be too much too soon.

I had no idea where the boundaries were; this was virgin territory for me – a conversation with someone *other* than Sinus?

With that they pulled me over to the side of the park and started teaching me to do an ollie.

'It's the best place to start. No better feeling than air

between your deck and the floor.' Dan had a soppy look on his face as he said it, the kind of expression your gran pulls as she puckers up at Christmas.

Emotional looks disappeared quickly as they talked me through it, though, and man, they were brilliant teachers. Within half an hour they had me flicking my board up into the air, and even though it was only a microsecond until my wheels hit the tarmac, I felt like I was flying.

They seemed pretty impressed too.

'Good skills,' chirped Dan.

'Aye. Took me ages to crack that,' agreed Stan. 'Few more weeks and you'll be on the half-pipe, no bother.'

This was going freakishly well. The stuff of legend. Remembering Sinus was watching, I turned to him, but he didn't look back. Well, he did at first, for a split second, before burying his nose and pencil back in his book.

'That your mate?' Dan asked.

'Er . . .'

Stan interrupted. 'I've seen that kid at school. Everyone reckons he's wired wrong. Just stands there and stares into space like some kind of fruit loop.'

What followed was a proper old school character assassination, the type I overheard about myself as I walked down the corridor, the kind that made me feel like the biggest outsider to ever enter the school gates.

They sniggered and pointed at him without a trace of subtlety, but for some reason I didn't set them straight, tell them he was all right, that he was my mate.

Instead I stood there silently as they ridiculed him, and even when Sinus looked back in our direction I still didn't speak up. Instead I put my deck on the floor and went back to practising my ollie, feeling a pang of guilt as Sinus gathered up his stuff and walked away.

'Want to meet some of the others?' Dan asked, once Sinus had slunk out of sight.

I should've said no. Thanked them for all their help and called it a day. I should've chased after Sinus. But I didn't, of course.

Instead I buried all thought of him and nodded like a dog in a car window. Naively, I followed them, feeling for the first time in my life like I'd arrived, like I belonged.

13

I lived at the ramp after that. Sprinted there after school and at weekends, made my deliveries in the quickest time possible. Anything to grab even five minutes pulling the tricks I'd been trying to master.

I had the ollie under control now, sort of, bending my knees deeply before springing both me and the board skywards. Within a month I was tentatively trying other stuff: shuvits, kickflips, heelflips, tricks I'd seen on YouTube but never dreamed that I'd actually attempt. Dan, Stan and the other lads that I'd met were brilliant, encouraging me all the time, tweaking the way I stood, how far I could balance before falling.

It didn't even matter when I wiped out spectacularly: they did too. Didn't matter that I was the smallest kid on the park by a distance either.

If anything, they reckoned it helped me.

'Pocket Rocket is Charlie.'

'Low centre of gravity. Helps him nail it every time.'

It felt weird to hear their compliments. I didn't really know what to do with them. It wasn't what I was used to. I listened harder than I ever had in my life, just in case they were meant for someone else. I mean, even Sinus, my only mate, wasn't exactly known for his random acts of kindness, so I felt myself growing every time they bigged me up.

It made a difference outside the skate park, too. I didn't feel quite as embarrassed walking into school every day, even though most kids had no idea about my new hobby. I started looking at people's shins instead of at the floor, even managed to speak up for myself when someone trod on me by my locker.

The only downside was Sinus. He disappeared. I looked for him every break and lunchtime, but he'd gone underground. And when I *did* track him down, he was quiet, blunted, lacking any kind of sharp comment or dig in my direction. Maybe he was jealous or hacked off at what I'd found: either way, things had shifted with him and I couldn't seem to do anything about it. I did try, out of guilt at how I'd idly watched the lads at the ramp badmouth him. But when my attempts were met with shrugs and silence I stopped trying so hard. There was too much fun to be had at the ramp.

Life at home was different too. Mum had thrown herself into a new course, something to do with hot-stone therapy. Sounded more like torture than pleasure to me. Either way, it meant more commitment, more nights at college, and we saw increasingly little of her.

The weird thing, though, was that she didn't look too happy about it. She was distracted, lines cobwebbing her forehead.

'Are you really *enjoying* this course, Mum?' I asked.

The smile I got back wasn't convincing. 'Wonderful,' she said. 'Why do you ask?'

'I don't know. It's not like you're bouncing about the place.'

That was true, but there was more to it than that. She hadn't fussed over me in weeks. Not really. Even when I nicked my cheek after a really gung-ho session at the park. She noticed it, course she did, barging into the bathroom as I cleaned it with cotton buds.

'You all right, Charlie, love?'

I felt my body tense, brain scrambling as it processed what the right answer could possibly be.

'Yeah, it's nothing. Got a bit rough with one of my spots, that's all.' I wanted to groan at the lameness of what my head had gifted me.

Normally that would've been enough to have her furiously Googling *facial injuries*, but not today. She didn't pounce on me to inspect the damage. Nor did she try to wrestle me into the recovery position. Instead her gaze seemed to ghost right through me, like she was looking at something far more important on the wall behind.

'You'll do your skin no favours, bursting them like that,' she sighed, before passing me the antiseptic cream from the cupboard.

I should've been relieved, or grateful, or both. But I wasn't. Something was up. Personality transplants didn't take overnight. Not in our house.

So for once, I was the one asking worried questions.

'You, er, all right, Mum?'

'That's very kind of you to notice, my love,' and she pulled me into her. I felt her body shake for a second. 'I'm fine. Really. Be even better if you left your poor face alone.' And that was it. She was off again, back on the bus to torture some other poor unsuspecting soul with a handful of pebbles.

'Is she really all right?' I asked Dad, in a lull between customers.

He was as helpful as ever, watching her until she turned the corner at the end of the street. 'You know your mum . . .' and he scuttled back to the kitchen sheepishly.

I chewed it over as I sat behind the counter, bagging up prawn crackers, feeling torn. Should I be concerned, or would that make me just as anxious as her? I squashed the urge in favour of a mild celebration. If this new approach gave me room to breathe, then it might give me more room to skate too . . . maybe it was all good, after all.

With Mum elsewhere, mentally and otherwise, I took full advantage. Pounding the pavements on the deck, deliveries flying in quicker and quicker, the tips piling up in the tin under my bed.

All the time, though, I could only think of one thing: the half-pipe. The ramp. The gargantuan beast that I desperately wanted to tame. I knew that if I could clobber that, then the respect of the others would be complete and I'd never be the king of clumsy again. The thought of it made my palms sweat.

How did I start practising on it in front of the others? I mean, they always said it didn't matter if you came off, but there were so many bodies on the ramp at one time . . . what would happen if I wiped everyone out? A multi-board pile-up. My head raced with images of frantic emergency crews dashing to untangle a dozen pairs of arms, legs and decks. Paranoia filled my head. It wasn't a good place to be.

I tried going down to the ramp after dark, when it was quiet. It was a real risk: Mum's timetable was unpredictable, so if I found her on the front counter I had to spin a line about homework at Sinus's. The lie stunk so bad I expected to leave surrounded by eager flies.

Still, she bought it, but only just, as she wasn't keen on Sinus or any of his family. I think she worried that I'd trip over one of their huge body parts and hospitalize myself.

Turns out my idea was a dud anyway. The lights in the park were way too dim to break the blackness surrounding the ramp, and without a whacking set of floodlights, there was no way I was going to learn. Not without ending up attached to a drip first.

It started to bother me, play on my mind more than it should. I was sketching ramps when I should've been embracing trigonometry. Teachers noticed and threats were made about letters to parents. It was properly bumming me out.

In the end I turned to my new mates, Dan and Stan, for help.

I saw them at school a lot, stood on the edges of their conversations, laughed when they did, nodded at what they said, but we didn't really talk much unless we were at the park. Which was fine, you know; they were older. Permission to breathe their air at school was acceptance enough for me.

They laughed when I told them I was nervous about the ramp.

'Mate! Course you're scared of it. That's the whole point. Without the fear there wouldn't be the buzz.' Dan was

68

wide-eyed as he spoke, like he'd necked a dozen Red Bulls through a straw in thirty seconds.

Stan was equally animated.

'Spot on. If you don't respect the ramp, it'll eat you up. There's nothing to worry about – you've got the best teachers on the whole park right here. We'll show you the ropes.'

I grabbed my board impatiently, geed up by their words.

'Whoa, whoa, big man,' gasped Dan. 'Not now. It's way too busy on there. Sunday morning. It'll be quieter, less mental. Less chance of maiming yourself.'

And with a nod and another handshake that moved so fast their fingers blurred, they launched themselves on to their decks, leaving me to count down the seconds to Sunday.

14

Sunday finally arrived. It wheezed towards me asthmatically, refusing point blank to take a hit on its inhaler, compounding my paranoia and fraying my edges still further.

I'd thought of nothing else but dropping off the top of the ramp for the first time. It occupied my every thought, awake or asleep.

As I scrubbed my teeth impatiently on Sunday morning, I stared into the mirror and cringed at the bags that hung beneath my eyes. I thought no one could look more tired than me. Until I saw Mum.

She was slumped at the kitchen table, every inch of her sagging as she clung on to a steaming cup of coffee. I asked her if she was OK, but it took three attempts for her to even hear me.

'Hard week at college?' I asked again, wondering if I should try sign language instead.

She tried a smile, but failed. 'No, no. Lots of fun. I think I'm getting the hang of it now.'

She wasn't herself. In fact she wasn't my mum at all. Some kind of personality abduction had occurred. I felt like I should check the back yard for signs of a UFO. There had to be some explanation for what was going on.

She looked so different. Like someone had slapped twenty years on her by scrunching up her face like a piece of waste paper. She rubbed self-consciously at her cheeks, the wrinkles fading momentarily before creasing again.

It wigged me out, course it did, because Mum never, ever looked defeated by anything. It wasn't in her vocabulary.

If anything or anyone had the audacity to challenge her or prove her wrong, she'd fight back. Nails exposed and voice raised if she had to. She might have been a monumental pain in the nether regions, but at least she had energy and enthusiasm. She wouldn't have endlessly gone to night school for the last eight years without it.

So what had happened? I had to ask.

'Are you *sure* you're all right, Mum?'

She managed to lift her eyes to mine, and they twinkled with affection for a nanosecond before fizzling out.

'That's very nice of you to ask, Charlie. And I am. I'm just a bit tired, that's all.'

'Why don't you go back to bed, then? I'll bring your drink up for you if you like?'

I felt bad suggesting it, and there was no way she'd accept, but it'd be easier to sneak out if she was back under her duvet. Easier on my guilt levels too if I didn't have to lie to get out the door.

'Maybe I will. Another half an hour wouldn't do any harm, eh?'

'Absolutely,' I nodded, though her answer made me want to probe further, dig into what on earth was going on.

We sat in silence for a minute. She looked like she might drown in her teacup if I abandoned her.

'Go on then,' I whispered encouragingly in her ear. 'Get yourself back to bed.'

I ushered her to the stairs, passing the drink into her hands as she climbed.

'I'm going out for a bit now. Be back for lunch.'

I braced myself for the inevitable question *Where to?* but it didn't come. Instead, she simply said, 'OK,' and closed the bedroom door behind her.

I frowned. It shouldn't have been so easy. There were no questions, no curfew, not even a searching look into my guilt-ridden eyes.

Bemused, I considered abandoning all plans, until anticipation started to bite again at my gut.

Shaking all other thoughts out of my head, I pulled on my trainers without undoing them and eased the front door shut.

As I hit the street, I glanced backwards once, to Mum's bedroom window, my heart leaping when I saw her figure filling the pane.

Was she on to me after all? Lulling me into a false sense of security?

I studied her gaze, heart settling when I realized she was staring absently into space. She looked so sad that I considered turning back. Fortunately, she shuffled away from the window and my guilt went with her.

Enough of all this. I had to get to the ramp quickly, before I changed my mind.

Dan and Stan were waiting for me, legs dangling from the top of the ramp as they chugged on cans of Red Bull. If bravery was an ingredient, then I'd buy a can or two myself because the park wasn't quiet at all – it was rammed.

There were already a dozen kids zipping up and down the half-pipe and at least the same again practising tricks around the pool. I felt sweat collect beneath my hoodie and tease me by sliding the length of my spine.

My two mates didn't look worried about it, though; they were too excited about seeing me drop in for the first time.

'Savour this day,' said Stan dreamily.

'Everyone remembers their first time,' agreed Dan. 'No matter what happens.'

I couldn't quite share their excitement; my guts were threatening to empty themselves at any moment. I made a note of the distance from the ramp to the grim, derelict toilets beyond the railings.

My nerve was failing, but I couldn't let it show. Not now I'd got this far.

'I reckon I'll have a bit of a skate around first. Practise my ollie, get in the zone.'

'Do it,' they agreed, watching as I zipped around the old paddling area, confidence spreading through me as I managed the dips and rises that had been my playground, but not a patch on the monster that was the ramp.

Slowly, the fear started to settle. As my momentum built

and the deck hugged my soles obediently, I reminded myself that I actually had some skills, so why shouldn't I give the ramp a whirl? If coming off was the worst thing that could happen, well, I'd done that a hundred times already and was still here. Still walking.

Yep, this was it. It was time.

Dan and Stan clapped their hands as we stood at the top of the half-pipe, looking down into the well before the ramp climbed again.

'This is it, little man. Life'll never be the same again,' grinned Dan.

'And, remember, don't try and pull no tricks. The aim of the game is staying on and feeling the buzz. Get them knees flexed, use your arms to balance . . . and have it.'

I stood there, beyond fear or excitement. Every emotion I owned swirled and whacked against my ribs. Nervously, I hooked the front of the deck over the edge, foot on the tail, keeping me upright. My eyes focused on the ramp, I waited for a lull . . .

It came seconds later, a clear path parting: it was now or never. Clumsy death or graceful glory.

I applied pressure to the nose of the deck, leaning forward with every bit of commitment I had. The floor fell away quickly, too quickly, and my panic levels grappled with the clouds above. I was falling, and in panic pushed my weight even further forward, feeling my guts lurch as the wall grabbed my wheels and propelled me on. Before I knew it I was climbing for the first time, wheels racing, a strange, excited, terrified howl blasting from my lips. I don't know if anyone else heard and I didn't care.

I was doing it. Having it. Flying. Forgetting every jibe, every loose elbow, every walk of shame I'd ever been subjected to. None of that mattered if I had this. None of it.

I remembered the bags of Dad's food that had balanced me for hours on end, felt the dull echo of every bruise I'd subjected my body to in practice.

Keep your focus, I said to myself. *Concentrate, balance, concentrate. Don't mess it up, not now.*

I thought of Mum too, of the guilt I'd carried around about hiding this from her. How I could get rid of it all now. Come clean and show her. Show her she could be proud instead of afraid. I could do this. Look at me!

Every turn became more important than the one before. Every bit of pressure I put on the board's tail to rotate was measured, precise, anything but clumsy.

At that moment, I wished I had a camera, something to preserve the moment when I was crowned king of the world.

And, as it turned out, someone *was* filming it – not for posterity or glory but to magnify my ultimate embarrassment.

As I dropped into the bowl for the umpteenth time, I saw something below me.

Someone that didn't belong there.

It wasn't another skater: there was no regulation hoodie or baggy jeans on show.

And there definitely wasn't a board under their feet.

There was just my mum.

With her hands on her hips and a face like thunder.

My heart stopped and the board thundered on, but not for long. The writing was on the wall and it read two simple words. GAME OVER.

15

I didn't dare open my eyes.

Not because I was scared I'd broken something.

No, the fear came from the last thing I saw before the board and I went our separate ways.

I didn't understand where she'd come from or how she'd known – all I knew was that it was definitely Mum towering over me. I could feel the anger radiating off her.

I jumped to my feet quickly, a minuscule part of me hoping that if I played the fall down, she might not see skating as four-wheeled Russian roulette.

One look at Krakatoa erupting from her face, though, told me I was out of luck.

I was about to kop for a massive rollocking, even by her overpowering standards.

'Charlie Han!' she roared, reducing the whole park to silence in only two words.

'What on EARTH do you think you're doing?'

'Oh, you know, just hanging out . . .' I ran out of lies before the end of the sentence, and changed tack, trying instead the dutiful son card. 'I didn't catch you, did I? Before that silly little fall . . .'

'Mate, you didn't touch her,' interrupted Stan from over my shoulder. 'You did this crazy Eskimo roll to avoid her. Ballsiest move I've ever seen. Especially without a helmet.'

Mum shot him a look of death, before upping it to one of extermination as she turned back to me.

'What are you doing here?' I asked her. 'You were off to bed. You should be there now. You're probably ill. Hallucinating and everything ...' I was rambling and knew it.

'Oh, I know what I'm seeing. Though, believe me, I wish I was dreaming. I couldn't sleep, could I? Thought a walk might clear my head. Shows just how wrong you can get things, doesn't it?'

I could see she was trying to keep a lid on her anger, but failing. Veins were popping on her neck. She didn't look tired any more.

'So? Do you want to tell me what's going on?' she hissed.

I felt a crowd start to gather as the others sniffed a domestic at worst, and, at best, the sight of blood. I half expected to hear a chant of 'fight, fight, fight' swell and engulf us. It didn't, though. They were clearly as terrified as me.

'Nothing's going on. I'm just hanging out. Skateboarding, that's all it is.'

My best casual voice wasn't cutting it, sounding strangled enough to summon every dog in the park.

'That's all?' she yelled, each word getting sharper. 'That's ALL? Are you insane? How long has this been going on and why on earth didn't you think to tell me?'

I panicked, not sure what the right answer was going to be. Did I lie and say this was the first time I'd tried it? Or claim ignorance and say I'd lost my memory in the fall? Which answer wouldn't lead me to being humiliated in front of the people I was most desperate to impress?

My brain formulated an elaborate, coincidence-laden lie, but at the last second my mouth betrayed me, spitting out the truth in one lame punctuation-free apology.

'AcoupleofmonthsnowIwantedtotellyoubutIthoughtyou dstopmeandIlovedoingthisandImreallygoodatittoojustask theotherstheylltellyouthesame.'

It sounded ridiculous, like the apologetic whine of a puppy who'd crapped on the rug before ripping up his master's sheepskin slippers.

All credibility, all hope, gone. I watched it disappear, so much faster than it had taken to gather.

Mum didn't care about that though. She didn't want to hear what Dan or Stan thought and, anyway, they were too gobsmacked, or terrified, to tell her.

'So you went behind my back instead, eh? You lied to me, for months. And where did this *thing* come from?' she asked, pointing at my board disdainfully. 'Did you steal it?'

For some reason, despite it being my own lies tripping me up, I started to get all indignant.

'Course I didn't steal it. I wouldn't do that, would I?'

'I don't know what you're capable of, Charlie. Not any more.'

'I borrowed it off Bunion.' I saw her roll her eyes in disgust. 'But I've saved up to add to it, from all the delivery tips I earned.'

This wasn't what she wanted to hear: it made her feel like my lies were even deeper and premeditated.

'You've been planning this all along, haven't you? You and your father. Trying to undermine me, when all I'm trying to do is look after you, keep you safe.'

The lads were crowded even closer now, eyes flicking between us as we spoke, like they were watching a game of verbal tennis. At times I thought I heard gasps as the conversation bounced between us.

'Keep me safe? You don't let me do anything! I've never been bowling, or biking when friends have gone. You wouldn't even let me go to the cinema with Sinus, cos you thought I might choke on some popcorn in the dark and no one would notice.'

'That was years a–'

Someone snorted behind me, but stifled it when we both turned and stared.

'And don't even mention Dad in all this,' I ranted. 'He hasn't got a clue what's going on. If he knew, he'd have come straight to you, because he knows what a NIGHTMARE you are!'

She looked ready to explode now, and I felt the crowd take a step back, fearing collateral damage.

'A nightmare, am I? I'll tell you what a nightmare is. A nightmare would be you falling off that death-trap and knocking yourself into the middle of next week. A nightmare would be sitting by your bed waiting for you to wake up, because you weren't brave enough to tell us what you were doing.'

She didn't pause for breath; it was like she had gills.

'But I'll tell you what, young man, you might think I don't let you do anything –'

'Well, you don't. All you do is wrap me up in cotton wool!'

'Well, you've seen nothing yet. I'll wrap you in so much cotton wool that you won't be able to move!'

And with one single shove, she moved me towards the crowd, which parted silently, all eyes staring at the two of us.

I dropped my head, feeling the ultimate shame when she ripped the deck out of my arms and carried it herself.

The silence was overpowering, broken only by the hammering of my own heart.

We walked another ten metres before the quiet was broken.

Broken by an avalanche of laughter from the ramp, which thundered towards us, covering me in seconds.

I'd gone from hero to zero in one minute. My humiliation was complete.

Prison life was tough.

Imagine Alcatraz with higher walls or Shawshank with shoutier guards.

Mum laid down the rules as soon as we got home, giving poor Dad as big a rollocking as me, despite it all being news to him.

He tried to escape back to the kitchen on several occasions, only to be blocked by Mum as she prowled in front of us. I was expecting her to turn our pockets out on the counter or delouse us before we were allowed near the kitchen.

It might sound like I'm making light of it, and I suppose I am. It felt important to find humour in the darkest moment of my already cloud-laden existence.

So we stood there for another fifteen minutes, Dad thanking his lucky stars the takeaway wasn't open yet. Taking a battering in front of your regular punters would've been an indignity too far.

Finally, as tears threatened to overtake anger, and having grounded me for what felt like the rest of my life, she stormed upstairs, leaving me to wait for Dad's reaction.

He still had a cleaver in his hand.

Despite how well I knew both him and his placid personality, I couldn't help but feel slightly nervous.

He wasn't livid like her though – more surprised and disappointed, which in some way felt worse. He stood there shaking his head as I told him again where she'd found me. It was the most animated I'd seen him in years.

'Not your finest moment, son.'

'I know, but it's not like she gave me any choice, is it?'

'She only wants the best for you –'

'Don't you dare say what you're about to say,' I interrupted.

He looked at me quizzically.

'Don't give me the line. The *she's your mum* line. Not today, Dad.'

'Then what do you want me to say?'

'Say you'll explain things to her. Tell her I'm only doing what everyone else my age does. Tell her she's being ridiculous, that she needs to let me grow up. Do my own thing without her running behind me with a cushion in case I fall over.'

It was probably the most I'd said to Dad in months, and certainly the most honest. He was the only one who could put a dent in Mum and her meddling. The only one she would possibly listen to.

I watched my words sink in, saw his face twitch as he processed what he could do to help. Maybe this was it. The moment he stepped over the line and took my side. Just this once. That's all I was asking.

'There's nothing I can do,' he sighed, running his index finger along the cleaver's blade.

82

'And that's it, is it? That's the full extent of your powers? Could you not for once grow a pair and help me out here? I'll do anything, Dad, just do me a favour, will you?'

'I don't think you've any right to ask favours of anyone right now. Not of me or your mum.'

'But you can see it, can't you? What she's doing to me? I'm a joke because of her. And it's getting worse. I can't go anywhere or do anything without her looming in the background. It's not right, Dad – she's not right.'

'She has her reasons you kn–'

'Does she? Really? Then you need to tell me what they are, because I haven't got a Scooby-doo why it always has to be like this.'

But it was pointless asking for answers. Despite the tension, despite the rollockings being dished out. To me it was the perfect time to get to the bottom of why all this was going on, but to them? I was persona non grata.

Dad's shutters came crashing back down in ten seconds flat.

'Well, you'll have plenty of time to work it out, won't you? What with being grounded.'

And that was that. Off he slumped, back to the sanctuary of his kitchen, but not before throwing a long, concerned look up the stairs, where Mum was either seething, or weeping.

I wasn't sure which was worse.

The duration of my grounding was vague.

Indefinite.

With no parole, and no TV, internet or console access

until I learned my lesson or turned thirty. Whichever came first.

I had visions of being an adult, sitting at the counter of Special Fried Nice in a jumper Mum had knitted me, still taking orders, still pedalling away on the rhino, dressed in fluorescent gear that had lost all its powers of reflection.

I was going to live a long, dull and cushioned life if Mum had anything to do with it. I might live to a hundred and fifty, but I'd never venture out of my comfort zone ever again.

Days lasted decades.

My head replayed the events of the last few months on repeat, but no matter how many different ways I thought of telling Mum honestly about the skating, the result would've been the same. There was no way she would have let me do it.

I suppose that should've made me feel better: that she'd *forced* me into lying, but it didn't help. I was banished to my room and my board locked up in a secret location. If she hadn't burned it already, or sealed it in concrete and dumped it in the North Sea.

The worst thing about the fall-out, though, was that Mum didn't seem satisfied with the punishment. If anything her fussing got worse.

'There are going to be some changes going forward,' she announced. 'Until you can be trusted, you'll be chaperoned to and from school.'

My stomach flipped. 'Eh? You're kidding.'

'Do you see me smiling?'

I didn't. Obviously.

84

'But what about Sinus?' I asked, even though we hadn't walked together in weeks. 'We always wait for each other.'

'Seeing as you got that death trap of a board from his family, I can only presume they were happy to deceive me too. You won't be spending time with him. Not if I can help it.'

'So Dad'll be dropping me off then?'

She waggled her finger knowingly. 'No. Your father will be too busy here to do that and anyway, you know what a pushover he is. I'll be picking you up and dropping you off every day. I'll be waiting at 3.40 p.m. in the teachers' car park.'

'But that's inside the gates,' I protested. 'Everyone will see you. I'll be a laughing stock.'

'Then you'll understand how *I* feel, won't you? You'll understand the humiliation.' She fixed me with an icy glare. 'In time I might trust you again, Charlie, but you will have to earn it.'

'So if I keep my nose clean I can go back to the ramp eventually?'

She slammed the worktop sharply, the whole building seeming to tremble in return.

'NO! You won't set foot in that skatepark again. Not if you want to keep me sweet. D'you understand me?'

I nodded, the pain of her punishment bruising me more deeply than any fall ever could.

If Mum was one thing, she was true to her word, and so the next two weeks at school were hell on earth. She insisted on the ridiculous chaperoning, parking closer to the school doors with every passing day, just in case I tried to slip past her in a bid for freedom. It didn't go unnoticed by the other kids – they laughed, pointed and banged on the car roof as I climbed in. I feared them surrounding us, rocking the car until they turned it upside down.

All right, I was feeling paranoid. *You* go through that level of indignity and not feel the same way.

But it wasn't unwarranted, the feeling of persecution.

News of the argument at the ramp had got around. Kids mocked me as I passed, others hunched over their mobile phones, shoulders shaking with mirth. At first I didn't realize what was going on, until one particularly huge year ten kid let me in on the magic.

'Mate, your mum is FIERCE,' he laughed. 'Someone filmed her slapping you down at the ramp. She's a monster!' I grabbed his phone as politely as I could, not wanting to look, but knowing that I had to.

And there we were, Mum going at me with even greater ferocity than I remembered. The sound quality wasn't great, but you could still hear her ripping shreds off me above the distorted howls of the others. What scared me most though, was the intensity in Mum's face. She had no idea that the skaters were laughing as much at her as they were at me. She was being eaten alive by her own anger, totally oblivious that dozens of phones were filming her every word.

I wanted the earth to swallow me whole.

How many others had seen the video too, or recorded their own version from a different angle?

How long till they had me doing a constant *walk of shame* as punishment? I felt my shins begin to throb nervously in anticipation.

Why was it that when the skating was going well, no one at school had a clue about me? I was still pretty much anonymous. But as soon as things went belly-up, everyone was in on the gag. The injustice felt overwhelming.

I was back where I started; in fact it was worse, because now I didn't even have Sinus on my side. I'd clocked him as the laughter followed me down the corridor, standing on the outside, watching the other kids take me apart, and he hadn't been laughing. But at the same time, he hadn't come over either, to tell me it would be all right, or even to take the mick himself. At least if he'd done that I'd have known we could be mates again.

It was a new low.

I couldn't have got any lower.

A professional limbo dancer couldn't have matched my minimal self-esteem. That's how low things were.

And do you know what?

Things were about to get worse.

It started with a text message that brought good news.

> I have an exam tonight, so can't pick you up. You are to
> walk home. DO NOT go NEAR the park. I am trusting
> you. Mum.

It was the best news in weeks, but surprising given the leash she'd had me on. I couldn't keep up with this new course of hers. The others had always been regular days, always in the evening, but this one seemed to be unpredictable, scattergun. I wondered whether she was doing it on purpose, to keep my paranoia levels so dangerously high that I wouldn't dare go near the ramp for fear of being rumbled again.

Whatever her motivation, I wasn't moaning about it. A day without being collected could only be a blessing, even if it meant walking home on my own.

But, as afternoon lessons crawled on, my brain began to itch as the skatepark lodged itself firmly in my thoughts. I hadn't seen or stepped inside it since the argument with Mum, but suddenly, with a sliver of freedom in front of me, I could think of nothing else.

At first I stayed strong, telling myself to get home as she had ordered. After all, I didn't even have a board any more. Even as I left the school gates, my intention was still to skulk slowly home. That was until I ran into Dan and Stan.

'Big man!' Stan hollered, despite being only a metre away. 'Where've you been hiding?'

'Hiding? I wish,' I answered. 'Everyone's got a photo of me on their phone these days. Didn't you know?'

'Don't take it to heart,' said Dan. 'It'll pass. Especially if you get yourself back to the ramp. Show off them skills again. Be the bigger man.'

I looked at them carefully, weighing up just how sincere they were or weren't being.

'You reckon?'

'Completely,' they echoed in unison.

'Everyone knows you can do it. One quick session without your mum there and that's it. Old news . . .'

My gut told me to follow them. My resolve started to crumble.

'But I haven't got a board, have I?'

But they weren't going to let that get in the way of me joining them. In fact they seemed even keener, practically begging me to follow them.

'Mate, people will lend you one. They'll be so chuffed to see you back.'

'Follow us down there. By the time you arrive we'll have a deck waiting. And a welcome party too if you're lucky.'

It was everything I wanted to hear. Everything. And it shouted so loud that I couldn't hear Mum any longer. There was only one place I was heading, and it definitely wasn't home.

It was brilliant to see the half-pipe towering in the middle of the park, as imposing and magnificent as it ever was. But in a way it gutted me too, reminded me how much I'd missed not just the skating but the acceptance I'd found while I was there.

The place was rammed, as it always was after school, bodies arcing and spinning all over the place. My ears were filled with the clatter of wheels on tarmac, the odd cheer and holler as someone pulled off something deadly.

And all I could think was, *It could've been me. Maybe it still could?*

I leaned on the railings, my body language like a lovesick fool, or Sinus zooming in on a dreamy newly built wall. A shout rang out from inside the park. Dan, smiling, waving me inside.

'What took you so long?' he grinned, as I stumbled through the gates, eyes flitting around for any sign of Mum hiding in the bushes. 'You know Harry, don't you?' He pointed to a lad next to him, huge peaked cap plastering his hair over most of his face. I could still see that he was grinning madly.

'Charlie! Where've you been, you animal?'

'Grounded by Mum,' I moaned, not wanting to sound like some snotty little kid, but failing miserably.

'What, all this time? It's been weeks. When will she let you off?'

'No idea. Could be months. Years. When I leave home and get a job probably.'

I noticed a few of the others had joined Dan and Harry

now. Stan, of course, but some of the other lads too who'd been there on the fateful day. I was shocked but pleased that they were happy to see me.

'Your mum is fierce,' said Stan, who offered no crazy handshake today. 'When did she get so crazy?'

I shrugged, though it felt weird to hear someone but me badmouthing her.

'Funniest thing I ever saw,' said one lad.

'She should be on one of them reality programmes. *Britain's Nuttiest Women* or something.'

Mum was suddenly the hot topic and a surge of jokes and insults rippled round the group, which was still growing. There must have been twenty of them joining in now, which only added to my unease.

'Don't know what I'd do if I had a mum like that . . .'

'I'd leg it. Get myself adopted . . .'

'Live with me gran . . .'

It felt like time to go, like I'd heard enough, but as I made to leave I realized I was surrounded.

I tried not to freak out, especially as they were all smiling at me. But they weren't happy smiles. They were 'something's going on' smiles. Smiles I'd seen before when people were about to rip the mickey out of me. Before I had to walk between them as their legs started swinging.

'Me and the lads were sorry about what went on,' Dan grinned, sounding properly pleased with himself. 'We'd heard through the grapevine that your mum had burned your deck. So we've got a couple of things for you. Things that'll sort you out. Get you back on the move while keeping your mum happy too.'

I didn't like where this was going, or the sound of the rumours they were making up. She might have hidden the deck, but I knew she wouldn't have burned it. Not really.

Sniggers rolled around, pinching at me.

'First,' said Stan, 'is this.'

And from the crowd, out came a board. Well, a deck. A scruffy, chipped plank of wood really, with no trucks or wheels, and certainly no design sprayed on to it. Even with a wedge of money and weeks of work, it was oceans away from the one I'd had. I didn't know how to respond. Look ungrateful and it could all start again. So I pushed out my chest and tried to look pleased with it.

'Wow. I don't know what to say. Really. You know, cheers. I'll take it home now. Get to w–'

'But that does leave us with a problem,' interrupted Dan, almost cracking up. 'We have to think of your mum in this. How she feels about you being safe. So we've racked our brains and come up with something special.'

Uh oh. Here it came.

'What is it?'

Stan stepped forward, wrapping an arm around my shoulder, but holding a bit too tight.

'Inspired by your mum, it is. Not exactly state of the art, but we reckon she'd still approve. Cos she was on about wrapping you in cotton wool, wasn't she?'

I nodded, knowing I'd been the one to suggest it first. Instinctively I tried to step away but came up against a crowd behind me. I was used to being towered over, but this was a whole new level.

'Well, that'd never work. Ironic, really, but cotton wool would rip soon as you fell off. But our solution? Foolproof.'

And with that, the sun disappeared as an army of limbs pinned me to the floor.

All I could hear was laughter and the sound of tape ripping from a roll.

Whatever was happening, I doubted it would be quick. And it certainly couldn't be good.

18

Fighting was pointless, but that didn't stop me. I wasn't trying to prove a point, didn't believe that I could force them off me.

I was just terrified: what else was I going to do?

There were so many of them pinning me down though, that I could barely flex a finger, let alone a muscle, so after intense bursts of struggling that got me absolutely nowhere, I gave up, concentrating on fighting the tears that wanted to escape instead. How far would they go? They weren't going to strip me naked, were they? I didn't even have the prospect of a teacher's interruption to save me. Not this time.

It wasn't like they were hurting me, having sly digs or anything like that, they were just laughing as they wrapped my legs in something that I couldn't make out through the endless bodies. I tried to lift my head to see but they wouldn't let me, blindfolding me as they moved up to my chest and arms.

I found myself longing for a good old-fashioned walk of shame. At least that way I could see when it would end.

The only things I knew was that I was hot, that they were having a wicked time, and that I wanted it to be over as quickly as possible.

94

The noise of the tape got louder until it was screaming inside my brain, so deafening that I thought my ears would burst. I could feel it binding something hot and suffocating to my head, the noise echoing so badly that I thought I'd pass out. I tried to thrash with my head, but an octopus of arms stopped me until soon the only parts of my face left uncovered were my eyes, nose and mouth.

There was a last muffled sound of delight as the tape stopped ripping, and one by one they stood back, allowing the sun to fall on me again.

Next came laughter, and pointing: phones were pulled out of pockets and photos taken. I was centre of attention, front and centre – exactly where I'd always wanted to be. I was being *papped*, I supposed, and I hated it.

What was it they'd wrapped me in? I tried to lift my arms to my face, but it was impossible. They'd trapped them tightly against my sides.

They'd mummified me in something: my feet, legs, chest and hands. They seemed to have made a helmet out of it too as my head was already sweating.

Was it cling film? It felt plasticky, but with panic and embarrassment engulfing me I couldn't be sure.

I fought to get to my feet but couldn't. My knees wouldn't bend and my arms were useless. Instead I rolled, or tried to, but even that was an effort. After rocking up some momentum, I felt my balance tip until I capsized on to my front like a human caterpillar, a hundred little popping noises bursting all around me. Another wave of laughter rolled over my head, and then I knew what they'd done to me.

Bubble wrap.

They'd covered me up in bubble wrap.

'Yeah, yeah, very funny. Take it off now, will you?' I begged through a mouthful of gravel.

They laughed their response.

I tried to stand again, bending on to my knees. Another round of popping followed, like firecrackers being set off at my feet. They were so amused they could barely stand up.

'It's really funny,' I gasped, trying to make a joke of it myself. 'Bubble wrap, I get it, I do. But please take it off – I'm baking in here!'

I found Dan and Stan in the crowd, my eyes begging them to end the game, but they were helpless, wiping tears from their stupid smirking faces.

With anger simmering beneath the bubbles, I tried again to stand, forcing my legs to bend against the padding. It took longer than I wanted it to, but eventually I felt myself rising from the floor, and was just about to step towards the exit when they pushed me back to the ground and rolled me across the park.

Every second, every rotation, was humiliating. Every centimetre I rolled meant more popping, and more popping meant more laughter. I couldn't believe what was happening, that Mum's comment could lead to this.

They toyed with me for another few minutes: more photos were taken, some of them queuing up to be snapped next to me like a fish they'd caught at sea. Strangely enough I found it hard to manage a smile for this photo album.

Eventually, when they finally got bored, they guided me

through the gate and pointed me towards home. As a parting gift, they taped the new board to my chest, just so I wouldn't lose it on the way.

'Hang on,' I begged. 'You're not going to leave me like this, are you? I can't walk home – it's miles!'

The final words came from Stan, who patted me on the back, bursting a few more bubbles in the process.

'We owe it to your mum, dude. You know that. She knows how dangerous skating is. All we're doing is following orders.'

And with a gentle shove my new walk of shame began.

It was actually less than a mile from the park to Special Fried Nice. I'd done the walk a hundred times in my life, and it had never taken more than ten minutes, but today, done up like a kipper courtesy of my 'friends' at the ramp, it was taking forever.

An apathetic sloth with a wooden leg would've made better time than me.

For starters, they'd wrapped me up so tight that I could barely bend my legs. I was reduced to walking in fairy steps. I dreaded to think what I looked like, but from the reaction of everyone I passed I guessed it was hilarious rather than terrifying.

People smirked, laughed, pointed and did huge double takes. One toddler cried before hiding under his mum's skirt, while the braver kids did what everyone does when they see bubble wrap. They popped it.

It was like being pecked by a flock of ravenous chickens. Every inch of me seemed to be under attack, even the wrap on my face got blitzed. I was like a tyre slowly being let down and there was nothing I could do to stop it.

The most annoying thing, though, was that while people were happy to deflate me, no one offered to remove the wrapping. One old lady that I begged for help grimaced before lacing into me with her brolly. It was the one and only time I was grateful for the padding.

I mean, what was wrong with people? It wasn't as if they'd taped my mouth up. They could hear me asking for help, so why wouldn't they oblige?

I was only halfway home when it all got too much. A group of ten-year-old hoodies had taken to walking behind me, picking me off bubble by bubble, until in the end I snapped, roaring in a voice that I didn't know I owned, words I barely knew the meaning of.

Did it work?

Not a chance.

Instead they swarmed on top of me, forcing me into the gutter, snapping the few bubbles that remained.

And the sad thing was that I just lay there and let them get on with it, hoping they'd get bored before all the pockets had burst. I had no fight left. Not for them, not for the kids at school. Not even for Mum and Dad. I was spent.

Fortunately, I didn't have to wait that long for the indignity to end, as a car screeched up beside me, horn blaring.

The kids scattered and the rear door opened, a pair of arms pulling me into the back seat. With a screech of tyres we were off, and as the hands pulled the bubble wrap from my sweating head, I had to hope the ordeal was finally over.

Although my mouth had never been covered, I still found myself gasping for air as the last of the wrapping was yanked from my head.

It could have been relief or shock that had me hyperventilating, not that it mattered. All I could feel was the sweat that had been trapped against my forehead tumbling down my face and on to the padding below. I felt like a burst water bed.

Slumped against the car seat, I swivelled to thank my rescuer, only to be confronted by the last person I'd expected.

Sinus. He may not have spoken to me in weeks, but here he was now, picking impatiently at the Sellotape round my wrist, like it was a run-of-the-mill thing to be doing.

'Interesting look you're rocking today,' he said without looking at me. 'Urban skateboard chic, is it?'

'Linus!' barked his mum from the driving seat. She peered at me through the rear-view mirror, a look of bemusement and concern on her face. 'Are you all right, Charlie, love?'

'Never better,' I answered, pasting on a smile. I liked Sinus's mum. She was sound. Interesting-looking, but I suppose she had to be with sons like Sinus and Bunion.

In fact, that's a bit of a lie, as I didn't really know what she actually looked like. Her face was always caked in so much make-up that I had no idea if she was a looker. I had to presume not.

She did that weird thing that some women do where they smear as much orange on to their face as they can, until it reaches their chin, where it stops dead, leaving a pasty neck beneath. Her head looked like a lolly on a stick: so sickly orange that I always expected a swarm of wasps to surround it in summer.

I liked her, though. Her smile might have been fluorescent red, but at least it was sympathetic.

'What's been going on?' she asked. 'You being bullied?'

'No, he always dresses like this after school,' deadpanned Sinus. 'Especially when he's trying to impress his new mates.'

'I'm sorry,' I gasped, not quite sure to whom or for what I was apologizing. After all, *he'd* been ignoring *me* too.

'Do you want me to phone your mum? Tell her what's gone on?'

'No,' I shouted, a bit too urgently. 'I mean, she's in an exam. She'll have her phone switched off.'

'Well, you'd best come back to ours then. We'll get you sorted out. You look like you could use a drink.'

I spotted my face in the mirror. It was as red as hers was orange, and no more appealing. I did need a drink, although I reckoned I had three pints of water trapped between the bubble wrap and my skin. Didn't fancy drinking it though.

Sinus harrumphed next to me, but still picked away at the tape. It meant he didn't have to lift his long nose and actually look at me. It suited him fine all the way back to his.

The towel was dripping by the time I'd dried myself off. The bubble wrap lay at my feet in a monumental heap.

'I think I preferred you with the padding on,' said Sinus, more sarcastically than ever.

'I look like a prune.' I showed him my fingers, which were shrivelled and puckered like I'd been in the bath for a day and a half.

'Am I supposed to feel sorry for you? Well, don't be asking for a hug, cos you're not getting one.'

I sighed. Why did it have to be Sinus who sorted me out, when things had been so tense between us? I knew there was a massive 'I told you so' moment coming.

'Are you still hacked off cos –'

'Whatever gave you that impression?'

'Let me finish, will you!' I barked. Too much had gone on today to leave me any patience for Sinus. 'Are you hacked off because the lads at the park laughed at you the other week?'

'Don't be ridiculous,' he scoffed. 'Do you really think I give a toss about any of their opinions?'

'Then is it because I've been busy practising? Is that it? Not involving you?'

'It's your funeral,' he shrugged.

Good grief, he was like a sulky toddler.

'Because if I have ignored you, I'm sorry. I suppose I might have got carried away with it all.'

'Whatever.'

'I got excited, you see. You would too, you know, if you had something you cared about, something you were good at.'

He jumped off his chair and straight down my throat.

'Who says I'm no good at anything? Who? And based on what? Anyway, how would YOU know what I care about!'

'Whoa, ease off, will you?' Sinus was fuming, doing this funny little dance of anger in front of me. It looked like he needed a pee. 'It's just . . . well, you've never told me about anything, that's all. You're my mate, but it's not like we talk about anything, is it? Not really . . .'

'Yeah, well, maybe I don't feel the need to shout about things I'm good at. Maybe it's enough for *me* to know. I don't need to feel popular, unlike some other people.'

All right. It was a cheap shot, but it was true. Hurtful too. I was sick of being the clumsy kid from the Chinese chippy. I wanted people to notice me for once. But look where it had got me. I couldn't tell Sinus that though, couldn't let him off the hook that easily.

'Well, I'm not like you. And anyway, it's not like you're happy, is it? Whatever it is you're so good at, it's not like it fills you with joy. You spend all your time these days with your nose in that dumb-ass notebook.'

A cringe flashed across his face until he shook it to the floor. I'd wounded him. I'd never so much as pierced his armour before.

'It may be stupid to you, but I know what's in it.' He sounded so immature I expected him to blow a raspberry at me.

'Show me, then,' I fired back. 'If it's so impressive, show me what's in it. Dazzle me.'

'Nobody looks in my notebook but me.'

He was driving me mad. And I wasn't up for it any more.

'Do you know what, Sinus? I'm grateful for your help today, I really am, but you're doing my head in. You sit there, all smug, laughing at me for putting myself out there, but you'll never do the same for yourself. You do realize what the other kids think of you, don't you?'

He shrugged like he didn't care, but for once I knew he did.

'They think you're a headcase. That your brain doesn't work properly. You stand there, staring at walls for hours on end like some kind of plank. I mean, doesn't that bother you at all?'

The words fell out of my mouth too easily. Never in my life had I ever been that direct with anyone. I suddenly worried I'd been way too harsh and backpedalled furiously.

'But I don't think you're weird, because you're my mate. So if there's something brilliant going on in that notebook, then show me. Cos if you're not prepared to show everyone, I am. Because that's what friends do.'

I saw his hand linger by his back pocket where the legendary notebook lived. But nothing came out. Instead he smiled and shook his head.

'Can't do that, Charlie. Not the book.'

I groaned and thought about leaving, but he stopped me.

'I'll do better than that. I'll show you properly what I can do. Full scale.'

He had this mad look of confidence on his face. He looked smugger than ever before, which given his normal, misplaced arrogance was saying something.

'Go on, then.'

Again, his head shook fiercely.

'Nope. I'm not going to tell you when. You'll have to wait. Keep your eyes open and you'll see it.' His eyes widened with excitement. 'Thanks to your little escapade today, you won't be able to miss it.'

In that moment, I wondered if all the other kids were right, that maybe Sinus's brain had fallen out of his nose when he was blowing it.

But there was something about the steel in his eyes that made me stick with him, tell him that I looked forward to it.

'Walk to school tomorrow?' I asked him.

'Nope,' he answered. 'Things to do tomorrow. Stuff to plan. I'll see you there.'

I'd undoubtedly stirred something up in him. So, without another word, I gathered up the soggy rolls of bubble wrap and headed first for the bin, and then for home.

20

Despite being annoying and way too smug for his own good, it was brilliant having Sinus back onside. The weeks that followed the bubble wrap incident would've been horrific to survive on my own. The ribbing after my public run-in with Mum at the ramp was nothing compared to this.

Kids laughed openly in my face, poems and songs were penned in my honour, portfolios of photos were downloaded and taped to every surface imaginable, even toilet seats. Nowhere was safe.

Camera phones were undoubtedly my nemesis. There were at least thirty different images available: you could've made a slideshow out of them.

In fact, someone did, and had it playing on the plasma screen telly that sat in the canteen. Never before had there been so much laughter about something other than the excuse for food on offer. I sat and watched through my hands, feeling my world end yet again as I rolled around the floor on screen, every inch of me popping and bursting.

Cue Sinus, cape practically billowing behind him as he strode towards the TV.

He got within a couple of paces before running into two gorillas from year twelve.

'Switch it off and we'll do the same to you,' one grunted.

Sinus cocked his head on one side and looked them in the eye. 'Interesting image,' he said. 'But it doesn't really make sense as a threat, does it? Why not just tell me you'll deck me if I touch it? Far more effective that way, isn't it?'

They looked at each other, completely baffled by this lesson in thuggery, before both cocking their fists in his direction.

Strangely, Sinus understood this threat clearly, and ran towards the exit, pulling the TV's plug out of the wall as he went.

I'd never seen him move so quick, especially when they threatened to pick him up by his nose.

They could've fitted a fist up each nostril with ease. Not that I bothered telling them myself; I was in enough trouble as it was.

Sadly the ribbing wasn't limited to the canteen. It started when I stepped inside the gates at eight a.m. and didn't stop, even when I was taking orders over the takeaway counter in the evening.

I had a nickname too, one to rival Sinus. But it wasn't the Pocket Rocket as it had once been.

Nope, I was now the Bubble Wrap Boy to anyone that knew me, and plenty that didn't.

Sinus and I hid our way through the school day like a couple of outcasts, trying to find humour in the new and varied ways they found to ridicule me, but every minute of every day physically hurt. Especially as I'd been so close, for once, to some kind of acceptance.

I felt their taunts whacking me on the head, pressure building, making me feel shorter by the second, but each time I was in danger of disappearing into the mud Sinus picked me up and told me not to worry.

'It could be worse – you could be our Bunion,' he'd offer, and that would keep me going to the end of break at least.

He was no less weird than normal though, still as obsessed as ever with his notebook and walls.

He became really fixated on one massive expanse of brick just outside the school gates, the side of a terraced house that overlooked the classrooms. It loomed large enough to remind me of the skate ramp, and was visible from pretty much every part of Bellfield Secondary.

It was, in short, *his* kind of wall, and so when some graffiti appeared on it, he took a particular interest in it.

Well, I say graffiti. At first it was just one letter, a huge, four-metre-high 'B', that had been crudely sprayed. Someone either had very long arms or a bloomin' big ladder.

'What do you make of that?' he asked, as he stared critically at it.

'What?'

'*That!*' He nodded, like he needed to debate the merit of it.

'What, the graffiti?'

'Is it graffiti?' he asked. 'Is that what you think it is?'

'Well, it's not the *Mona Lisa*, is it? And unless we're living on Sesame Street, then what's the point? We all know what a "W" is.'

He didn't say anything else about it, just stared at it over his shoulder as we walked away, pausing for one last look before we turned the corner.

'Is it all right if Sinus comes in for a bit?' I asked Mum from the other side of the counter.

She eyed my friend suspiciously, Sinus returning her stare with the most innocent one he owned. He knew Mum didn't warm to him, but as usual he didn't care.

'We've homework to do. A project.'

'He can for me,' chipped in Dad, eyes watering as he skilfully diced the biggest onion I'd ever seen.

Mum glared at him, leaving Dad to shrug and continue chopping.

'As a trial, yes,' she said eventually. 'But don't think I've forgiven you or your brother for lending our Charlie that skatingboard.'

I cringed at her mistake.

'Skateboard.'

'Whatever. Death trap is what it was. A noose on wheels.'

She shook her head and pulled her scarf round her neck.

She must have guessed what had been going on for me at school those last few weeks. Maybe this minute softening was her way of telling me she was sorry for what she'd caused? Doubtful, but in my position you'd be scrabbling for consolation too.

'You off to college?' I asked.

'Not tonight.' The look of sadness returned to her face. 'Night off. But that doesn't mean I'm not busy. Those kitchen cupboards don't fill themselves, you know.'

This was excellent news. It meant we had a good hour of peace before she returned to fuss Sinus out of the door.

'Straight down to your homework,' she said as she walked away, finger pointing at us both. 'No PlayStation!'

'Of course,' I replied.

'No way,' agreed Sinus.

She walked out of the door and we turned to each other.

'PlayStation?' I asked him.

'It would be rude not to,' he agreed, and followed me up to my room.

What followed was a very happy but all too short fifteen minutes of *Call of Duty*.

Mum didn't know I had that game, of course. There was no way she'd let me have something so violent. She was reluctant to let me play *FIFA 2013* for fear of me pulling a muscle. I'd picked up *COD* second-hand on eBay, then chucked the packaging away the second it arrived, hiding the disk inside a case from an old Muppets game. Mum didn't think Miss Piggy could do me any harm, you see.

Every time we got stuck into our mission, though, the phone would ring. Not the one in the takeaway, weirdly, but our home phone. People never rung us on that number. Mum was always on her mobile, taking calls about her latest school course, but the home phone? Well, it needed dusting.

Nobody answered the first time it rang. Dad wouldn't have heard it above the woks and there was no way I was interrupting my game for someone trying to sell us double-glazing.

I ignored it the second time too, but by the third attempt I was starting to feel paranoid.

'Do you think it's Mum checking up on us?' I asked Sinus.

Sinus didn't take his eyes from the screen, but launched into this full-on impression of her, his voice all shrill and panicky. It sounded nothing like her, but it was funny.

'Have you finished your maths yet?' he squealed. 'Don't sharpen your pencil too much. Lead poisoning's a killer!'

I didn't mind *him* ribbing her, unlike the idiots at the ramp. From him it was funny, plus he'd shut up if I told him to. Eventually. So I joined in (not that it was much of a stretch to pretend I had a high-pitched voice) and we went off on one, dreaming up ridiculous ways of hurting ourselves. We must have sounded bonkers, aping her voice like that, but we didn't care – it was great to laugh for once. It'd been a while.

The phone started a fourth time and rang for ages, then a fifth time. I couldn't ignore it any longer and, still chuckling, I walked into the hall and picked it up, forgetting to stop talking in Mum's voice as I spoke.

'Hello,' I shrilled.

A voice came back at me immediately, a breathless panicky voice that didn't belong to Mum but to another woman.

'Oh, thank goodness you're there, Shelly. I couldn't get through on your mobile. It's Pauline from Oakview. There's been a setback with your Dora. I'm afraid she's had another one. Another seizure.'

I had no idea who this woman was or what she was talking about. But in the two minutes that followed, everything I knew turned on its head.

21

For the first time in my teenage life, I was pleased my ridiculous squeaky curse of a voice had never broken. After two minutes of impersonating Mum, though, my throat was starting to sting like a bunch of nettles. But there was no way I could give up, there was still stuff I had to learn.

The conversation so far had gone something like this.

Me: 'A seizure? Dora?' I fought to think who on earth she was talking about.

Pauline: *long pause* . . . 'Er . . . yes. She's been much brighter all day after the episode yesterday, and we'd hoped the new medication might settle her down. But she started convulsing about an hour ago.'

Me: *brain wanting to explode in confusion, voice slipping lower.* 'Convulsing?'

Pauline: *longer pause* . . . 'You know, shaking, fitting. Like she does whenever she has one of her seizures.' *Pause* . . . 'Shelly, are you OK? You sound . . . strange. Are you ill?'

Me: *voice higher and shriller than ever.* 'No, no, I'm fine, I was just . . . having a nap when you called. I must have been sleeping heavily. I feel a bit spacey.'

Pauline: 'Oh, I'm sorry. You don't *sound* like yourself.'

Me: 'I'll be fine in a minute. So is, er . . . Dora OK now?' I was on the verge of giving up the pretence and hanging up, but my hand refused to obey my brain. 'Can she come to the phone?'

(Maybe if I heard her voice it might make more sense.)

Pauline: *sounding bemused, like she's talking to a complete idiot.* 'Not really. But she's fine now. Honest. She's sleeping. And besides . . . well . . . you know, it's not like she can tell you about it herself, is it?'

My heart stopped but my brain whizzed a hundred miles an hour. So whoever Dora was, she couldn't speak? What was going on? Was it some kind of bad joke from one of the kids at the park? I mean . . .

Pauline: 'Shelly, are you still there?'

Me: *sounding shellshocked* . . . 'Yes.'

Pauline: 'Please don't worry, love. I know she's your sister . . .'

Me: *HEAD EXPLODES IN DISBELIEF.*

Pauline: '. . . but it's honestly no worse than the one yesterday, and she's resting now. The doctor's looked her over and he's confident that with the right balance of medication she'll settle right down again. There's no need to rush over here. Maybe *you* should try and sleep too. You still sound . . . tired.'

Me: 'I am. It's just a shock, you know.'

I wasn't lying either. Though 'shock' didn't quite cover it.

Pauline: 'Course it is, but there's nothing to worry about. We'll see you as normal tomorrow, eh?'

Me: 'Yes. OK. Bye.'

I put the phone down gently, then staggered, zombie-like, into the bedroom. Where on earth did I start with this one?

For once Sinus was silent. No sarcasm or put-downs, just the sound of the room filling up with my far-fetched story.

'Whoa,' he finally said. 'That is trippy.'

'Do you reckon it's a joke? Someone from the skatepark?'

'Mate, bubble wrap is one thing, but this is something else. No one could make up stuff like this!'

He was right, but I couldn't believe it was true either.

I mean, Mum having a sister? She was an only child. I thought back as far as I could for the sketchiest of memories of an auntie, someone more laidback and normal than Mum. Someone that stuck up for me against her clucking. But there weren't any. I hadn't even met my grandparents. They'd died before I was born; there had only ever been Mum.

'If this is all true, then why wouldn't she tell me?' I asked Sinus. 'Why keep a secret like that?'

'Beats me.'

'And what about Dad?' I was starting to get angry now, confusion boiling my blood. 'I mean he must know about it. She can't have kept it a secret from him too, can she?'

Sinus shrugged, looking for a second like he wanted to get out of this madhouse.

'I'm going to ask him,' I shouted, jumping to my feet. 'Have it out with him.'

Sinus grabbed me and pulled me back to the carpet.

'Don't do that. Not yet. Imagine if he doesn't know. Imagine if she *has* kept it from him. He'll go mental. No, we need to check this out first. Do some digging around.' He grabbed my laptop and opened it up. 'What did you say the name of the place was again?'

My mind went blank.

The name had a tree in it, but I was blowed if I could remember which one.

I sat there looking gormless.

'Come on!' Sinus looked aghast. 'You can't have forgotten that already?'

'Some complete stranger has just told me that I've got an auntie that I never knew about. Apparently my mum and possibly my dad are the biggest liars walking the planet. And apparently I'm as naive as they are devious. So forgive me if I can't remember that the name of the hospital was Oakview . . . It's Oakview. Oakview.'

I put my hand to my mouth in relief, as Sinus hammered the name into Google.

'Oakview,' he read. 'It's a nursing home. Long-term patients . . . blah blah blah . . . twenty-four-hour care . . . specializes in head injuries.'

'Where is it? I asked, mind racing.

He scanned the screen. 'Old town. By the fishing museum.'

'Right.' I was back on my feet again. 'Let's go.'

'Where?' he asked dimly.

'Where do you think, idiot? Oakview.'

'But your mum'll be back soon, won't she?'

I looked at the time. Mum always filled a trolley to the ceiling, so I reckoned if we moved fast we still might be safe.

'We'll have to find transport,' I thought out loud.

'It's two buses to get there.'

That would never work. We had one option. It wasn't a good one and Sinus was going to hate it. But it was all we had.

22

I pedalled like the wind. Well, like a gust . . . or maybe just a gentle breeze.

OK, I pedalled as hard as I could without damaging myself.

Getting the rhino to move was difficult at the best of times, but with Sinus wedged into the basket on the front it was ridiculous.

He made an almighty fuss when I showed him the trike, but he was so nosy that the thought of being left behind was worse than the idea of embarrassing himself. With a final grumble, he clambered into the box, legs dangling over the handlebars. I might have been smaller than him, but there was no way he could get the wheels turning.

If I hadn't been so mega-stressed, I would've laughed at him. He looked ridiculous. All he needed was a blanket wrapped round him and he would've been a dead ringer for ET.

We could've done with some other-worldly powers: someone to lift the bike into the air and propel us there at jet speed. Instead, all I could do was grit my teeth and power us on as best I could.

We arrived after about twenty-five minutes, both of us ready to collapse: me with exhaustion and Sinus with cramp. He rolled about on the floor like a footballer. I was tempted to kick him while he was down there, but resisted the urge – I'd undoubtedly need his help. Instead I pulled him to his feet and told him to man up.

Oakview was a big place, must have been a hundred years old, all pillars and plaques. The building sat in the middle of a huge garden, with ancient trees and stone benches dotted about. Even though the oaks were enormous, they couldn't block the sight of the sea about a mile away.

'Nice gaff,' said Sinus.

'Huge,' I added. 'Think we'll find her?'

He shrugged. 'We can try. Reception's that way.'

I paced towards the house, suddenly realizing I had no idea what I was going to do when I got there. I mean, how do you ask for directions to your long-lost auntie's room? And what was I going to say to her when I met her? Would she even know who I was? That I even existed?

Suddenly it all felt too much. All I wanted to do was climb on the rhino, creak my way home and climb into bed. But something stopped me.

The thought of Mum's face the last few weeks, the creases and emotions scratched deep into it. All the worry that I thought had been about some stupid massage course, when it had actually been about Dora – whoever she was.

I thought about all the years she'd kept up the act, the courses she'd invented to keep reality from me, all the skills she'd made up just to be here. I couldn't begin to count the number of journeys she must have made.

I had a hundred questions burning up in my head and had to believe that the answers lay inside that building. Even though the possibilities running through my mind scared me, I had to listen. There was no alternative.

So, still without a clue about what to say, we pushed through the double doors and into the reception area.

It was cavernous, the size of our flat. More like a stately home than a hospital. The only reminder was the smell – that artificial and antiseptic odour that makes you tense as soon as you step inside.

It seemed calm, with gentle music piping in through speakers that I couldn't see. It was like being sung a lullaby.

The only thing that wasn't calm was the nurse behind the front desk. She was trying to do three things at once and failing at all of them.

She was on the phone, the cord wrapped twice round her body as she struggled to feed paper into a printer. She babbled into the receiver in a language neither I nor Sinus understood. It was either medical talk or swear words so sophisticated we hadn't encountered them yet. After the abuse I'd suffered that past month, I had to believe it was the former.

Even though she was failing at what she was already attempting, she insisted on trying to drink a cup of juice that sat by the printer. A long curly straw poked from the cup and each time she dipped her head to it, she managed to poke herself in the eye. Comedy gold, but I wasn't in the mood to laugh.

She didn't notice us for a couple of minutes, eyes rolling in frustration when she finally did. The last thing she needed was a couple of kids to deal with too.

Instead, she finished the conversation in her own time then tried to untangle herself from the phone cord, knocking over her drink in the process.

More highly medical terms spat from her pursed lips.

I pulled a wad of tissues from the box on the desk and dabbed at the spill, knocking the liquid closer to her printer.

'Yes, yes, thank you,' she snipped, grabbing the tissues from my hand. 'I *can* manage.'

Sinus shot her a look that said, *Are you sure?*

If I really did have an auntie living here, I hoped this wasn't her nurse.

She pushed the liquid around the desk for another minute or so, huffing and puffing until, with a final flourish, she threw the soaked tissue into a bin, took a deep breath, pasted on a really flimsy smile, and sighed. 'Now, boys. What can I do for you?'

No sooner had the words passed her lips than a siren rang out. The kind you hear in World War Two movies when the Nazis are about to blitz London. She appeared so panicky that I thought I should dive under the nearest desk. Grabbing a microphone that sat on a small stand, she hollered two words that ripped through both the speakers and our eardrums – 'CRASH TEAM!' – before vaulting over the desk and towards a door to the right, knocking her glass over again.

'I'll be back, boys. Wait right here,' she hollered over her shoulder.

At that point I was obediently looking for a chair, but not Sinus. Instead he raced after her, catching the door she'd dashed through, just before it locked behind her.

'What are you doing?' I whispered.

'We've got forty minutes until you have to be home. I'm trying to find this auntie of yours before your mum locks you up for life.'

He was a genius. A snotty, irritating, big-nosed genius. What would I do without him?

Without a second's thought we piled through the door and up the stairs in front of us. Dora was in here somewhere. All we had to do was find her. And quick.

23

Every corridor looked the same.

I was beginning to forget which ones we'd already explored, panic rising as my ticking watch echoed louder and louder, bouncing off the high ceilings.

'Anything?' I stage-whispered to Sinus.

He shook his head and peered through the next door, banging his nose on the window as he did it. There wasn't time to laugh.

It would have helped if I knew what Dora looked like, but I had nothing to go on. Not her age, hair colour, anything. I didn't even know if she was older or younger than Mum – she might've been adopted for all I knew. We could be looking all night.

It felt weird looking in on the patients, like I was planning to rummage through their stuff or something. What made it worse was just how incredibly ill they were: most were in bed, some sleeping, while some lay staring into space. The more active ones were propped up in chairs, watching the telly unfold in front of them. It didn't look like they were registering the flashing images, never mind enjoying them. I started to worry about how ill Dora might be. These fits she'd been having: what did they mean? What if seeing me made her have another one? What would I do? I started to freak out, my thumping heart threatening to call the search off, when Sinus yelled way too loudly from the bottom of the corridor.

'I've found her,' he shouted, but he wasn't smiling. 'She's here.'

My feet flew down the hall quicker than any board could. Sinus stood, face fixed to the window, breath steaming it up.

'You sure?'

'Positive.'

I barged him aside a little too roughly and wiped the window with my sleeve.

And there she was.

It had to be her.

Had to be.

She looked like a broken bird version of my mum.

I don't know why, but I'd seen her in my head as a big woman, overweight and loud, maybe even wild-looking. But Dora was none of those things.

She was tiny, toothpick thin. Her limbs more bone than flesh, skin stretched so tightly over her joints, I was worried it could rip at the slightest movement.

She was so different to Mum, but I had no doubt they were sisters. One glance at her eyes told me that. They burned with the same fire. It was like seeing Mum in fifty years time.

She was a bit scary to look at, like a puppet on an old TV show, but despite the slight repulsion (and, as a result, guilt) I couldn't stop myself pushing through the door and into her room.

'Keep a lookout,' I whispered to Sinus, who stood, chest out, bodyguard-style, at the door.

Her room was tidy, but full of stuff. She looked like she'd lived there all her life, compounding the enormity of the lie.

There were shelves in every corner, crammed with pottery figures and animals. Elephants especially: all of them with their trunks facing the window.

My eyes flicked restlessly over every surface. I wasn't interested in the bric-a-brac. I was looking for something that reinforced what I already feared, and I found it on the table next to her bed.

A brown wooden picture frame, Mum, Dad and me smiling out of it. I remember it being taken, minutes after leaving the pantomime about five years ago. We'd laughed harder than we ever had, before or since. Mum looked completely happy, not a trace of worry anywhere on her face. I'd always loved it for that reason. Hoped one day I might get an encore.

The presence of the photo stunned me, shouted without doubt that Dora was real, that there'd been no mistake in what I'd learned on the phone. The truth forced the fizzing adrenalin through the soles of my feet as I flopped on to the edge of her bed. After gazing at the photo for another moment, I lifted my eyes to meet hers properly. She was looking at me. It made me jump.

'Hello,' I blurted. 'I'm, er ... Charlie. Your nephew. Apparently. Remember?' I lifted the frame next to my cheek and tried to recreate the smile in the picture. I was acting like the one with the head injury rather than her, so I put the frame down and smiled apologetically.

She said nothing. Just drilled her gaze deeper and deeper into me. I wondered if she *could* talk. Had to try and see.

'I didn't know about you.' I leaned forward, trying to look relaxed when really I was bricking myself. 'Not until this afternoon. They called to say you were ill, which was a bit of a shock as I didn't even know you were alive! Imagine that, eh?'

Her mouth twisted across her face, followed by a stream of spit and a strange noise somewhere between a croak and a scream. Was she trying to talk to me or call for help? I hadn't a clue, had to watch as the drool dangled helplessly from her chin.

There was a box of tissues by her chair, so I offered her one. She looked at me like I was crazy. She could move her arms and hands, they were twitching around on her lap, but they didn't seem interested or able to reach the tissue.

Slowly, I leaned in to wipe her mouth. I don't know why I was hesitant, it didn't look like she would bite, but I just wasn't used to people who were so . . . I don't know, ill. And anyway, this wasn't getting me anywhere. Not in terms of answers.

As my hand reached her, she lifted her head slightly, offering me her wet chin.

'Thanks,' I said, wiping the spit away gently. 'That's better, isn't it?'

She said nothing, just stared.

'They told me you were ill. That you've been having seizures. Bad ones.' It seemed a bit crazy talking to her like this, but I didn't know what else to do. 'What happened to put you here? Is it something to do with Mum, is this why she worries so much?'

Another stream of dribble ran to her chin but I scooped it away before it fell.

'I just wish I'd known about you, you know. I would've come earlier if I had, honest.'

At that moment, I thought I saw something resembling a smile, and in that moment my heart leapt. Unfortunately, I didn't get a chance to look again, as Sinus piled through the door and almost on top of me.

'Oh no,' he gasped. 'Oh no, no, no, no, no . . .'

I was on my feet already. 'What is it? Is someone coming?'

He was out of breath, despite only running ten paces.

'Not anyone,' he gasped. 'Not *anyone*! Your mum!'

24

Within seconds, Sinus and I became the biggest clichés walking the earth.

Knowing we couldn't exit via the door without Mum spying us, we pranced around the room, yelping and getting in each other's way, much to my aunt's delight. Her laughter was the biggest evidence of life within her fragile frame yet.

Dora's bed wasn't made for hiding under, too many levers and mechanisms, and if Mum got the sense someone else was in here then I knew it would be the first place she'd look.

Or possibly the second, after the wardrobe, where Sinus had leapt in sheer panic.

Neither of us was getting points for originality, that was for sure.

It wasn't exactly spacious under the bed: it had taken a lot of frantic wriggling to hide myself completely, but somehow I managed it (thank the Lord for my tiny bones), wedged up against a metal pole that adjusted the bed's height. If they decided to mess with that, I was in danger of being skewered, kebab-style. Still, it'd make it easier for Mum to roast me, wouldn't it?

The door flew open and my mum's voice cut in, only just audible above my thumping heart.

'So who *did* you talk to on the phone?' she asked, the normal panic in her voice.

'I've no idea. I should have realized it wasn't you when the questions started. I'm so sorry, Shelly. I'd tried your mobile umpteen times, so didn't know what else to do.' I recognized who this was. Pauline, the woman I'd spoken to on the phone.

'Don't worry,' said Mum. 'You must have rung the wrong number.'

'But why did they pretend to be you, then? I just don't understand it. There's some sick people out there.'

Yeah, I thought. You're talking to one. A devious, conniving one.

I didn't like this Pauline and her endless questions either. What was she? A nurse or a private eye? I lay there, thinking how she should be devoting her time to sorting Dora out instead of piecing everything together so neatly for Mum.

The footsteps stomped closer, stopping at Dora's chair, a metre from my head.

I had no idea how they couldn't smell my panic.

Mum began to speak to her sister, her voice softening instantly, a tone that was new to my ears.

'Hello, Dor,' she cooed. 'Sorry I didn't get here earlier. I didn't know you were ill again, did I? How are you feeling?'

I slid my head in line with the very edge of the bed frame. Risky, but it got their faces to sneak into view. It was weird to see them, two sisters, almost nose to nose. It was like they were both looking into a fairground mirror.

It killed me, everything about it: that Dora was sick, that I hadn't known, that Mum was so sad, but also that she was devious enough to lie to me. All of it. I felt my shoulders tense as tears started to gather, but told myself to quit it. I didn't know enough, or trust Mum enough to give me the truth if I gave myself away. Besides, there wasn't room to cry under there. Not without drowning in a salty puddle of my own making.

I had to hold it together, wait until Mum left and then work out what to do. Then I could be angry or sad or confused: whatever helped.

'So how severe was the seizure?' Mum asked Pauline, her eyes never leaving Dora.

'I won't lie to you, Shelly. It was a prolonged episode. The sort we'd hoped the new medication would control, but it looks like we'll need to reassess. Find the right dosage.'

Mum rubbed her eyes. She looked terribly tired.

'I'm so sorry, Dor,' she whispered. 'You don't deserve this.'

Dora made her own sad sound, like she was agreeing with her.

'It should be me lying there, shouldn't it? Not you.'

My head was on the verge of exploding now. I didn't need another bombshell on top of what I was already trying to process. What did she mean? Why should it be her? I was so confused I had to bite my lip to stop myself from asking why.

'So what have you been doing today, hmmm?' Mum asked, as she tucked a blanket over Dora's lap. 'Have you watched some telly?'

A stream of noises came from Dora, words I guessed, and

although they made no sense to me, they definitely did to her, and to Mum too, it seemed.

She listened patiently, watching as her sister's hands twitched in her lap. 'Really?' It was like she was answering a toddler. 'And how was that?'

Dora's words got harsher, louder, her arms waved like a windmill.

'OK, OK, calm down, my love. There's no point getting yourself in a state. I'm here now, aren't I, and the doctors will sort out these problems, I promise.'

But I didn't think Dora was telling Mum about the seizures: Dora was telling her sister about her nephew under the bed and the big-nosed kid in her wardrobe.

Not that Mum understood this time. Instead, she clicked into overbearing mode. This was the Mum I knew.

'Now calm down, Dor. There's no point in getting yourself all wound up. Not after the day you've had.'

She had stamina, though, did Dora. Wouldn't stop grunting and waving for the next fifteen minutes as my legs slowly went from cramping to sleeping to a deep comatose state. I dreaded to think how long Sinus would be able to keep quiet for, unless he'd fallen asleep in there. I had to presume he had, dreaming weirdly about the world's biggest wall.

I thought Mum would never leave. That in the end I'd be given away by my growing hair snaking from under the bed and up her crossed legs.

Mum sat for aeons, sometimes talking, sometimes silent. They were obviously very comfortable in each other's company, that was for sure. In the end it was Pauline who saved us, a bleeping on her pager causing her to turn back to Mum.

'The doctor's finished his rounds now, Shelly. Do you want to try and talk to him about Dora's meds?'

Mum nodded enthusiastically and gathered her stuff up, pausing to kiss her sister gently on the forehead.

'I'll be back in a bit,' she whispered. 'Try not to get yourself overexcited.' I recognized the force in her voice.

Dora grunted once more, as the door closed behind Mum.

No sooner had it shut than the wardrobe door flew open, a sneeze from Sinus almost blowing it clean off its hinges.

'Bloomin' dusty in there,' he moaned, using a coat hanging inside to wipe his nose. 'I've been holding that in for quarter of an hour.'

'Sounded like it,' I groaned, as he pulled me from under the bed, my shoulders scraping against the frame as I emerged. 'I thought she'd never leave.'

'Me neither. Starving, I am. You got anything in that basket on your bike?'

I didn't answer. Food was the last thing on my mind. Instead I crouched in front of my auntie and tentatively took her hand gently. Her bones crackled beneath my fingers. It was like holding on to a piece of hundred-year-old tissue paper.

'Sorry about that, Auntie Dor,' I whispered, shivering at how strange those words felt. 'We didn't mean to freak you out. I'll talk to Mum, I promise. Sort all this out. You don't have to worry about a thing. Just get yourself well.'

The words sounded hollow, stupid. This was clearly as well as she got.

'I'll come back soon. Next week or something. OK?'

She groaned and let her head fall back on to the headrest, eyes already closing. She was tired. And I suppose I should've been too. But there wasn't time.

We had to get on the rhino and back home pronto, as I knew now what I had to do. It wasn't a great idea. But then again, it was all I had.

I had to talk to Dad.

25

The wok hit the ground a second after I said Dora's name.

It spat angrily in my direction, annoyed at the size of the secret I'd dug up. Noodles scattered across the floor. I expected them to spell out the word 'panic', the emotion etched across Dad's face. His expression told me everything: that he knew all about her, that all of it was true. I felt the last disbelieving cells in my body collapse and held on to the door, tight.

He didn't move at first. His mouth twitched as if it wanted to form words but had no idea what they were.

Then he did something he'd never done before.

In the middle of his rush hour, he turned off each of the cooker rings in turn, the woks hissing their disappointment, this time at him.

I loved watching Dad cook, it was the one time he came alive, the one time he looked truly – or even vaguely – happy. He was octopus-like, spinning a dozen things at once, knives, woks, pans, graters. He was never fazed when orders came in thick and fast. He just stepped up through the gears. That was when he was most alive.

But now, with the mention of one name, he fell apart. The hands that could dice an onion in fifteen seconds fiddled nervously with his apron strings, failing to untie them.

'Charlie,' he bumbled. 'Where did you hear that name?' Maybe he hoped I was asking about another Dora. One who didn't mean a fourteen-year-old lie.

'On the phone this afternoon. Some woman called. She thought I was Mum. She said Dora was ill, which was strange, because I had no idea who she was talking about! Turns out Dora is Mum's sister. Imagine that, eh?'

Dad said something in Chinese that I presumed was a swear word. I hoped it wasn't an explanation as he'd have to do a lot better than that. I suddenly wished I still had Sinus with me, that I hadn't insisted he jumped off the rhino as we passed his house. He was so pumped by the mystery of it all that he hadn't looked at a single wall all the way home. Instead he came up with elaborate, implausible and highly inappropriate reasons for Mum hiding Dora away: that her sister had been possessed by aliens or lost her mind in a top-secret pharmaceutical experiment. I chose not to listen: whatever the reason, it made me feel sick.

Back in the kitchen, Dad walked slowly towards me, trying to put his hand on my shoulder as he passed. Irritably, I shook him off. I didn't want a hug or calming down, I just wanted answers. Today. Now.

But Dad was in no rush. Instead, he sheepishly despatched the delivery guy without anything to deliver, flipped the sign on the door to closed, took the takeaway phone off the hook and pointed me towards the lounge.

'Let's sit,' he said, suddenly looking as old as Dora had.

I followed him, flopping down on our saggy sofa as he perched nervously beside me.

'I've been expecting and dreading this conversation for a long time,' he sighed, rubbing at his eyes. I could feel the heat from the woks pouring off him. 'Tried to work out in my head what I would finally say when you found out.'

'And?'

'I don't know what to say. I never worked it out. What do you already know?'

I was fuming now, more confused and angry and hurt than I thought it possible to be.

'Oh, you know, just the usual stuff that happens on a Wednesday. That I have a long-lost auntie, that she's seriously ill, that my parents have lied to me ALL MY LIFE!'

He nodded and looked me right in the eye.

'Yep, all of that's true.'

There was a calmness to his voice that I couldn't cope with. It was opposite to everything I was feeling.

'Well, were you ever going to tell me, or was all this planned? Was it easier for me to find out from a complete stranger than for you to tell me the truth? I mean, what was going on in Mum's head?'

'She's your mum,' he said, for the millionth time in my life. It was one time too many, the time that broke the camel's back, even though I had no clue what a camel was doing here anyway. They weren't on Dad's menu.

Tears escaped from my eyes, which only made me angrier. I wanted to be livid, not weak.

'But that's not good enough!' I yelled. 'Do you really think that's enough? That it explains how she – you – could possibly hide something as important as this from me?'

'Course it's not enough.' He looked close to crying himself, which was hugely worrying. A sentence was a huge achievement for Dad, but tears? Really? 'I don't know where to start. How to explain to you.'

I jumped to my feet, heading for the door. 'Then I'll go back to the hospital and ask her myself.'

'The hospital? You've seen Dora?'

'Seen her? We chatted, we're best mates, off bowling next week to get to know each other better. I even hid under her bed while Mum talked to her.'

Dad leapt to his feet and guided me back to the sofa.

'Wait, Charlie. Before you go rushing off and upsetting your mum, just wait . . .'

'Upsetting Mum!' I hollered. 'Upsetting Mum? What about me? What about how I feel? I think I might be a teeny bit peeved myself. Can't we think about that for a second!'

'Course we can. I'm just trying to keep the peace here. Trying to work out what to do for the best.'

'Well, the best thing would've been telling me about this years ago. The best thing would've been honesty. Instead of hiding an auntie behind flower arranging lessons and plastering diplomas, because the last time I checked, they weren't the same thing.'

Dad looked gutted, like I'd belted him around the head with a wok. He was way out of his depth.

'I don't know what to say, son,' he sighed, and I believed him, I really did.

'Just tell me the truth, Dad,' I begged. 'That's all I want to know. The truth. All of it.'

So that's what he gave me.

26

'Dora was thirteen when the accident happened,' Dad sighed. 'Two years younger than your mum.'

I thought of my tiny auntie, perched in her chair, of how much older she looked than Mum or Dad. Twenty years at least.

'They were very close. Always had been. Your grandma and granddad were . . . strange people. Never showed either of their kids much love, so Dora and your mum looked after each other. Know what I mean?'

I didn't, but it wasn't important. I just wanted him to go on.

'They did everything together and as a result didn't have a lot of other friends. They didn't need them when they had each other.'

My legs were bouncing nervously on the sofa, shaking us both.

'Dad, this is all very nice, but what happened?'

He coughed nervously, clearly not wanting to go on, but he had no choice.

'It was an accident. A stupid accident that could've happened to anyone.'

I made a circular motion with my hand: *Come on, come on.*

'They only had one bike between them. Your grandparents were too tight to buy them one each, and as a result Mum used to carry Dora everywhere on her crossbar.'

I thought of Sinus crammed into the rhino's basket and felt a bit sick. Maybe I didn't want to hear this after all.

'Your mum was ferrying them both to school one morning, and they were late as usual, no one had bothered to wake them up. Mum was really going for it on the bike, but because Dora was sat in front of her, she didn't see a pothole in the road. The bike hit the hole and both girls hit the pavement. Dora first, Mum second, one on top of the other.'

Every single centimetre of me cringed. The scene unfolded in my head, but I didn't want it there, especially as I knew what was coming next.

'Mum was OK, just grazes to her legs and arms, but Dora had taken the full impact, and she didn't have a helmet on. No one wore them back then.'

My head was full of the steel rhino, how cripplingly nervous Mum had been when she gave it to me, the demands she'd made about helmets and lights and stuff. It all started to make sense.

'Dora didn't wake up for a long time, Charlie. Months. The doctors weren't sure if she ever would. They could see that her brain was still active, but didn't know how badly it had been damaged.'

The room was completely still. My legs had stopped bouncing and all I could smell was soy sauce wafting from Dad's clothes.

'What happened to Mum after the crash?'

'We hadn't met then,' he sighed, 'so I only know what she's told me, but she blamed herself completely – for going too fast, for not making Dora walk, for not seeing the pothole. She took all the responsibility on her shoulders and carried it everywhere.'

'But Grandma and Granddad ... They must have told her it wasn't her fault?'

Dad shook his head. 'They were strange people. Hard. Were more interested in Dora after the crash than before it, and blamed Mum. They had so many chances to make her feel better, but never did. As a result, your mum blamed herself more and more.'

'So that's it? Dora's been in Oakview ever since? That's, like, twenty years.'

'Almost. There was one other hospital before your grandparents died, but after they passed away Mum decided to move them both away. She was paranoid everyone in the town knew about the crash, and was convinced that everyone blamed her. It upset her so much that she moved here, miles away from all the prying eyes, and found Oakview for Dora, knowing it would use up every penny her parents left behind. We met a few months after.'

'But she told you about her straight away, right?'

'Nope. Not until the night I asked her to marry me.'

'So she lied to you too?'

Dad looked mildly cross. 'No, she didn't lie to me. She just didn't know how to tell me. What you have to understand is how guilty she feels. Her parents had told her so often that it was all her fault that she believed it. She thought if she told me I'd run a mile.'

'But you didn't.'

'No, of course I didn't. I accepted her for who she is.'

'So why didn't she tell me too?'

'Charlie, I wish I had ten pounds for every time I've asked her to. We wouldn't be living here, that's for sure. Your mum is complicated, and proud and scared, so scared of what everyone thinks of her. The only way she could deal with it was to bury it from everyone, including you.'

'But she must have known that I'd find out in the end.'

'I know that and so do you. But she refused to believe it. I gave her my word that I'd keep her secret. It was wrong of me, but I did.'

I felt weird, like someone had stuffed me full of truths that I didn't want to hear, truths that didn't fit inside me. It was the most Dad had said to me in my whole life, and I wished it could've been about something else, but at least I knew Mum was wrong on one thing. He *could* speak as well as he cooked.

'So what do we do now?' I asked, still angry but sad as well, about everything.

'I wish I knew,' he sighed.

'I'll speak to Mum when she gets back.'

'No, don't,' he gabbled. 'Not tonight. Let it settle.'

'You don't want me to lie about it too, Dad, do you? Cos I don't think . . .'

'No more lying. I just need time, and so does she. Dora's been so sick lately that it's eating her up. Let Dora settle, then I'll tackle your mum, I promise.'

'You really will?'

He crossed his heart with his rough, burnt fingers and smiled.

'Absolutely. And in the meantime you need to think what'll make you feel happier. Anything you want, son, I'll do it for you.'

There wasn't anything I wanted, except for all this to be a dream, and I knew Dad couldn't sort that out. So instead I gave him a hug, feeling his body shake slightly against mine, making me squeeze him that bit harder.

As we finally parted, I thanked him for telling me everything and meant it.

Not just for telling me the truth, but also for volunteering to play a part in the mental plan that followed.

27

School rocked. I loved it. Everything about it.

Well, it beat being at home anyway. It beat how I felt when I had to spend time with Mum.

I didn't know how to react when she was around me. I was this mad, fizzing cocktail of feelings. I didn't know it was possible to feel angry, confused, sad, envious and pitiful at the same time, and I definitely didn't enjoy it. I felt like a can of Coke that was continually being kicked down the stairs.

Fortunately she was so wrapped up in her 'night class' that she didn't realize how I was feeling; it was like no one but Dora existed.

Two weeks had passed since the seizure that led me to her, but according to Dad things at Oakview were no better. The fits had continued almost daily and the doctors were starting to worry about Dora's heart, whether it could cope with the pummelling it was taking. There was an increased chance of a stroke too. I know I'd only met her once, but I didn't think her cracked shell of a body could cope with that. I tried to find positives in it all: at least I *knew* now, at least Dad was apparently trying to work everything out. But at the same time I was feeling a real sense of urgency. Like, if Dad didn't do something soon, it might all be too late.

With all the gloom at home, I almost skipped to school every morning. Even though I still took the occasional *walk* courtesy of the other kids, their blows bounced off me now, nothing in comparison to the bullets that were fired back at Special Fried Nice.

Sinus kept me sane too, although something strange seemed to be happening to him. *Quelle surprise*. At first I thought Dora's story had been too much for him to hear, but it wasn't that. He was acting, well, borderline normally.

I caught him having conversations with kids around school, actual proper conversations where they spoke and he listened, and vice versa. They looked as surprised as me. Rumours went round of him being the first living recipient of a brain transplant, but when he heard them he just laughed them off. No signs of bitterness or resentment. Nothing.

The whole notebook thing was different too: it still got whipped out, course it did, but not all the time. He'd walk without his nose being thrust into it; he'd look around him, chest out, nodding at other kids as they walked by.

It was weird, different, scary.

He wasn't the only thing changing at school either. There was something else going on too, something that *everyone* noticed.

There was graffiti going up everywhere. Wherever there was space there it was. It had started on the big wall by the yard, with that massive 'B', which over the next week turned into 'BW', then 'BWB'.

And that was the maddest thing about the graffiti: it was always those same letters appearing. They were sprayed differently on each wall, varying colours and types of lettering, but appearing so often that everyone would stop and talk about them.

It was weird how three simple letters started transforming the walls, making the building look like it had a heartbeat of its own. There wasn't a single kid who didn't stop, take it in and raise their eyebrows in approval.

Teachers weren't so keen, though. Emergency assemblies were called to discuss the graffiti.

'Vandalism!' hollered our head, Mr Peach. 'Mindless vandalism.'

He challenged the guilty party to 'stand up and be judged', but no one did, even though they would have got a standing ovation from every kid in the hall. This was hero territory: whoever the artist was, they would be beating the opposite sex off with a stick!

The penny dropped on the day a new design appeared: and not just a simple 'BWB' either. This one was awesome. The first thing that hit you as always was the letters – two metres high in green, red and blue spray paint.

But to their left there was the silhouette of a boy in profile, pursing his lips as he blew a succession of small bubbles over the letters. The bubbles weren't moving, of course they weren't, but they were sprayed with such intensity that they seemed to shimmer in the light as you walked past.

Not that people *did* just walk past. EVERYONE stopped and stared. Me included. I was mesmerized by it. Only stopped staring when I was ushered into class.

I came back at break though, then at lunch and the end of the day, brain itching hard without me quite being able to scratch it.

'Take your interest, does it?' a voice behind me asked.

I spun to find Sinus, looking properly pleased with himself. He must have finally figured out how to make a million from bottling his own snot. He'd been trying long enough.

'It's amazing,' I said. 'The coolest thing. Must have taken them ages.'

'Him, not them,' he said, sighing.

'Eh?'

'There is no *them*, only *him*,' he bragged. 'Well, me, actually.'

I was staring too hard at the wall to take in what he said at first, but finally my brain caught up.

'Eh?' I grunted again, Sinus-esque in my vagueness. 'What did you say?'

'I said the artist works alone. Always. Because anyone else's input would merely water down my vision.'

'*Your* vision?'

He flicked me a look that said *Work it out, imbecile*, and I did, all the evidence falling into a completed jigsaw that simply said: 'Sinus is the artist.'

His unsettling fascination with bricks, then the notebook and the endless scribbling ... It all made sense now, well, kind of. I still couldn't quite believe that my mate, my idiotic awkward mate, could have this kind of talent. But why would he lie?

I jumped on him in excitement, hugging him, trying in

vain to lift him into the air. From a distance it must have looked like Concorde had made an unsuccessful comeback.

'Get off me, will you?' he blushed. 'I hoped this might make me irresistible, but not to you!'

'Why didn't you tell me?' I said. 'Why hide something as awesome as this?'

He shrugged, trying to look cool again, although the tips of his lips were curving into a full-on beaming grin.

'Told you I'd do it when I was ready, didn't I? *And* that I'd surprise you.'

'Well, you've definitely done that! Aren't you bricking it that Peach will find out? And what's with the "BWB"? It's everywhere.'

'Peach don't bother me,' he bragged. 'Not when it's in aid of a mate who's desperate.'

I felt myself deflate slightly. After all the abuse he'd dished at me for wanting new friends, here he was wooing some kid in year eleven, or, knowing, Sinus, probably some girl.

'Who is it then?' I tried not to sound hurt.

'Have you even looked at this?' he laughed, forcing my head back in the wall's direction.

'Course I have. All day pretty much.'

'And have you not noticed what's going on in it?'

'Yeah, there's a kid. And there's bubbles. Loads of them.'

'And which *kid* do you know of who's had a lot of bubbles in his life lately?'

I looked at him blankly and he stared right back. Deeper and harder, until ... WHAM! It lamped me right between the eyebrows.

Not the end of his nose, but the answer.

Me. He was talking about me. Course he was. I'd had more bubbles than a king-size jacuzzi.

'This is for me? But why? I don't get it, Sinus.'

He answered in a voice that was meant to be Yoda, but sounded more like his gran on helium. 'Many questions you have. Time this will take. But trust in Sinus you must.'

Impatient, I punched him. 'Talk properly, you nugget.'

He punched me back, but at least talked properly. 'Oi! Don't hurt the talent,' he grunted. 'Especially when you're my muse. I am doing all this for you.'

'So you said, but what do you *MEAN*?' I was bemused to the point of exploding.

'Operation Bubble Wrap, mate. By the time I'm finished, you'll be almost as cool as me.'

Ten minutes before, that comment would've been a massive disappointment. A crushing blow.

But now? With Sinus's new skills?

Maybe, just maybe, he might be on to something.

28

'It's fair to say you're a laughing stock right now,' Sinus began, helpfully.

This didn't sound like much of a plan so far. Not one that would help anyway.

'But it doesn't have to be that way,' he continued.

Phew. That sounded more like it.

Sinus whipped a piece of dog-eared paper from his pocket. It looked like it had been there for weeks, including three trips through the washing machine.

'I presume you've seen this?'

'Depends what it is. Strangely enough, I've seen a few things lately. I use these things called eyes – you might have heard of them?'

He unfolded it with a flourish. I strained to make out the lettering, all melded and morphed into a language that could have been ancient Sanskrit, but equally could have been drunken gibberish.

'What is it?' I asked, twisting my head to one side to try to decipher it. 'Some kind of holy scripture or something? Cos I don't really believe in that stuff.'

He cuffed me with the paper impatiently. 'And you call

me vacant? Have you not looked at the notice boards around school, seen what's coming up in six weeks' time?'

I shrugged. I'd spent most of the time lately looking at the floor after the other kids knocked me to it.

'This is your shot, Charlie. Redemption. This is your chance to reclaim the cool you'd built up. This is what the "BWB" is all about, why I've been spraying it everywhere.'

I didn't get it. He might as well be speaking Swahili for all the sense he was making.

'It's *Skatefest*, you idiot. A festival of skating. Tricks, half-pipe comps, races, all sponsored by a skate company.'

'Where?' I peered at the poster, but still couldn't make anything out.

'On top of the London Eye, you tool. Where d'you think? In the park, of course! They're building a whole day around it. Stuff for everyone. Fair rides, fireworks, the full monty.'

I knew what he was saying, but couldn't see how it helped me. I didn't have a board, and even if I did Mum wouldn't let me out of her sight. Oh, and there was the small fact that all the kids had humiliated me last time I stepped foot on the ramp.

I tried to suggest all these small factors, but he waved them away dismissively.

'Mere details,' he scoffed. 'Point one – you have a board. The apes gave you one on the day they mummified you.'

'But it's rubbish,' I protested.

'Then we'll do it up. You have savings. Use them! Point two – your mum is so distracted by all things Dora that she wouldn't notice if you rode out of the takeaway on the back of an elephant, plus your Dad promised you ANYTHING to make you happy. Dude, that's like a golden ticket. Why you haven't tapped him up for every PS3 game known to man, I don't know. But use him – get him to help keep the secret. It's not like he hasn't kept one from you . . .'

He was right. It felt weird to use Dad like that, but he *had* promised.

Sinus wasn't finished. 'And point three. They may have got stuck into you that day at the ramp, but that wasn't cos you couldn't skate – it was down to your mum being weird. You can skate – it pains me to say it, but you can. You may be the Bubble Wrap Boy at the moment, rather than the *nice* nickname they'd gifted you, but we can change all that, reclaim the name, make it something cool, something to be proud of.'

I looked around at the walls, covered in his art. The design was amazing, but I still wasn't sure if he was right.

'I don't know, Sinus. It all seems a bit unlikely. Aren't they going to laugh me off the ramp as soon as I step foot on it? And what about Mum? If this festival's as big a deal as you say, then she'll see the posters. And, if she does, then she'll be suspicious. You know what she's like.'

Sinus fixed me with an evil look. 'I can't believe you're saying this after all the grief you gave me. You gave me both barrels for not showing off what I'm good at, and here you are, coming up with every excuse you can to not do something you love!'

'But it's different for me.'

'Yeah, it would be, wouldn't it?' He turned on his heel, threatening to leave. 'Cos you think you're better than me – you always have. But I'll tell you something, Charlie Han.

I'm going to keep putting the designs up there. Not because I want them to *like* me. Just so they'll finally notice that I've been sticking two fingers up at them for years.'

Blimey, he meant it. Suddenly he had all these crusading morals that I never knew about.

'Plus . . . if I get a girlfriend out of it, then even better! I have needs, you know.'

Ha! That was more like it.

'But trust me, Charlie. By the time I'm done, "Bubble Wrap Boy" will be the most uttered words in the school. Now if you don't want to make the most of it, then fine. That's up to you. But I'll tell you what – you'll never have as good a chance as this again. So think about it, eh?'

And he prodded me roughly on the shoulder before slinking off to scope out a new wall, leaving me with an awful lot of thinking to do.

29

I had no clue what to do.

Sinus's plan was huge. And exciting and potentially game-changing. But it came with huge risks too. Especially when you factored Mum into it. I was tiptoeing around her still, studying her every facial expression for evidence that Dad had told her what I knew, but all I got was the same mixture of glacial annoyance and distracted worry.

Did I dare go ahead with Sinus when there were already way too many secrets? I'd tried to tackle Dad about Dora again but got absolutely nowhere.

'When *are* you going to tell her, Dad?' I demanded.

There was a different answer every time I asked.

'Once Dora's settled down.'

'When the specialist has assessed her.'

'When hell freezes over.'

'When the takeaway wins a Michelin star.'

All right, the last two were exaggerations, but it felt like there was always a better reason than the best one of all. The truth. And after two more weeks of waiting, I decided that if Dad wasn't going to front it out, then I was going to go for Sinus's plan.

And Dad was going to be an accomplice.

I hit him with it when Mum was out (presumably hospital visiting).

The teatime rush was over and he was wiping the surfaces down, buffing them into a mirrored sheen.

'You said you'd help me,' I said quickly, before I could change my mind.

'Sorry?' He looked surprised to see me.

'You said if there was anything I wanted, anything at all, that you'd help me. Remember?'

'I do,' he replied. He already looked nervous and he hadn't even heard what I was after yet.

'I want to get back into skateboarding.' It wasn't until I heard the words out loud that I realized how much I meant them. So much so it physically hurt.

'You do, do you?' His tone gave nothing away.

'More than anything. And there's a competition coming up. So I need you to help me, Dad. I need you to get me back on the board.'

He looked like I'd asked him to steal the crown from the Queen's head.

'But I don't know anything about skating, Charlie.'

'I'm not asking you to train me. I just need you to cover for me, keep it from Mum if she asks where I am.'

He shook his head so hard it blurred.

'I can't do that, mate. You know how she feels

about it. She'd lay me out on this chopping board if she found out!'

'But you promised, Dad. You said you'd do anything.'

'And I will, except that.'

I had my reaction planned, and although I didn't want to carry it out I had to convince him that I would.

'OK.' I shrugged, like I didn't care. 'I'll tell Mum what I'm going to do myself. Right after I ask her about Dora.'

Dad went white.

'Play fair, son.'

'What? Fair like you two did? I'm not the only one keeping secrets, am I? I'm a novice compared to you two.'

He had no answer to that. There wasn't one.

'What do you need me to do?'

I stared at the sky outside; there was another hour of light clinging to it.

'Nothing yet. But I do need you to close up early.'

'I can't do that, Charlie . . .'

'Not till nine. And anyway it's Tuesday. Nobody wants your food that late on a Tuesday. No offence.'

'I think I'm about to be *more* offended by what you're about to involve me in.'

'So you'll do it?'

'This time, yes. But if there is a next time, I need notice. Time to get someone to cover both the kitchen and my back.'

'Thanks, Dad.' I laughed. 'You'd better have your car keys ready. Soon as it gets dark, *we* get started.'

The headlights worked a treat. With the full beam on, they lit the ramp perfectly. There was no issue getting the car close enough; couples had been using the park for a crafty roll in the back for years, so Dad simply edged the front wheels up to the fence and flicked the beam on full.

He wasn't happy about it, though. At first he sat and gripped the steering wheel, knuckles turning white, then blue. But after a couple of minutes it was too much for him and he joined me by the ramp.

'For god's sake,' he groaned, 'don't fall off, will you?'

'Can't guarantee that,' I grinned, checking the excuse of a board that the other lads had gifted me. 'That's half the fun.'

'Your mother will kill me if she finds out about this.'

'Then you're a bit stuck aren't you, cos I'll dob you in if you don't help me.' I would've asked who he was most scared of if I'd thought the answer was me. We both knew that wasn't the truth.

We shared a grin. 'Must be dreadful being a dad, eh? All these moral conundrums . . .'

'What do you think?'

I didn't answer. Instead I rammed the board beneath my feet and pushed off, feeling a thrill as it rolled beneath me. I'd forgotten how brilliant it felt. How at home I was on one.

The board wasn't as good as my old one, obviously. I'd modified the plank they'd landed me with, but the wheels still didn't run or turn as quickly. It was OK for now, though. Maybe once I had Dad fully on board, I could persuade him to tell me where my real deck was. If he even knew.

I pushed myself around the park, the car's headlights sending long, freaky shadows bouncing off the pavements.

I took the dips and rises of the old pool slowly at first, feeling my confidence grow until, after about twenty minutes, I was attacking them, feeling the buzz of air between my deck and the floor.

At first I thought I was getting too excited, making little whooping noises and gasps. Until I realized it wasn't me. It was Dad, unable to stop himself out of sheer dread.

'Careful now,' he begged as I zipped up a slope. He was even standing funny, mimicking my crouch on the board himself, like he was riding it. He looked ridiculous. I told him so.

'Hey, Dad?' I grinned, when my legs were finally feeling tired. 'Why don't you have a go?'

'I don't think so, Charlie.'

'Go on. I must have got the love of it from someone. So maybe it's you and you just don't know it.'

I didn't expect him to give in quickly, but there was no way he was getting off the hook. He still had plenty of payback heading his way, starting right here. So after ten more minutes of ribbing, cajoling and eventually cold, hard threats, I forced him to stand uneasily on top of it, arms snaking round me for support.

'What do I do now?'

'Well, you row, don't you?' I laughed. 'What do you think you do? You stand on it and push with your foot.'

I knew it wasn't that simple. Had weeks of bruising to prove it, but there was no way I was sharing that pearl of wisdom. Instead I watched him lurch and wobble just as I had, arms waving maniacally when I finally got him rolling along.

'Too fast. Too fast!' he yelled at first, although after a short while he started to relax and risked the briefest of grins before careering on to his arse.

I smiled too. Couldn't remember the last time I'd seen him smile about anything but his food or his kitchen. Decent memories of him away from his woks were way too few. I hoped he might recognize that too. Even if he was bruised beyond belief by morning.

I tortured him for a good while, long enough for him to start panicking about the car's battery running flat, which seemed a good enough reason to stop. Stranding ourselves first time out wasn't an option.

'Thanks for tonight, Dad,' I said as I pulled him off the tarmac for the twentieth time. 'Couldn't do it without you.'

'It makes me nervous, Charlie, all this.'

'I know it does. Me too, but that's why I have to do it. Can't be scared forever, eh?'

He glanced up at the ramp. 'I'm glad you're not going on that tonight.'

It towered above us both, winking at me, daring me to set foot on it. I shuddered at the thought of what had happened last time.

'Me too. I'm not sure either of our nerves are up to it yet.'

Dad breathed out noisily in relief.

'Next time, eh?' I winked at him.

He nodded, knowing, unfortunately, that there *would* be a next time.

'I can't wait,' he said, pulling me close and squeezing, as he guided me back to the car.

30

I should've been happier. I knew that. I didn't want to be an ungrateful little turd, not when I had a best mate cooking up the comeback of the decade and a dad doing every unreasonable thing I asked of him.

I just couldn't help it. It just all felt a bit . . . overpowering. The plan, the sneakery and, of course, the simple fact that I was still living in the middle of the HUGEST lie imaginable.

Skating was the only thing that kept me sane.

While I was on the deck, you see, my brain rested. It forgot to wrestle with images of Mum at the ramp, or Dora sitting broken in her chair.

Once the board was hidden away it was a different story. My head flooded with too many emotions: guilt, anger, jealousy even, that I'd been cut out of something so important.

It felt like everything I knew had been thrown into the air, and all I could do was run around like an idiot, dodging all the jagged lies as they crashed down around me.

The truth distracted me, my head dropped to the floor at school, leaving clumsy dumb-arsed Charlie to do his worst again. And when I messed up, the hyenas surrounded me.

I didn't notice how long the tunnels were any more, though. Kicked shins stopped stinging after a few minutes – the ache Mum had caused made me want to double over all day long.

Being in her company brought my confusion to the boil. I'd promised Dad I'd give him more time, but trying to act normally around her was impossible. I just wasn't as good a liar as she was.

'You at college tonight?' I found myself feeding her a lot of questions, knowing the answers would be lies. It wasn't like I expected her to suddenly blurt out the truth; it was more that I wanted to reinforce in my own mind just how angry I was with her.

'Oh, yes,' she replied, the picture of calm.

I watched her for giveaway signs: eyes flicking nervously, the rub of an ear, even an uncomfortable cough as another whopper passed her lips. But there was nothing. Not a flicker.

It made me wonder what else she wasn't telling me. Were there bodies hidden under the floorboards? Her parents, perhaps? Maybe they'd got on her wick one day and she'd bludgeoned them with a couple of splintered chopsticks.

All right, I know I was being silly, but it summed up what my head was doing to me.

Not that she noticed.

'What about you, Charlie? What's going on today?'

I paused. The truth burned my tongue and I felt the most overwhelming desire to breathe fire and tell her I was going to spend it skating. That way I could start a row, that way I could goad the truth right out of her.

'More toast?' Dad interrupted, getting right into my face, eyes wide, half pleading, half threatening. He knew how close I was to blowing. Knew he'd be the one left with a dustpan and brush to clean it up if it did all go south.

I was pleased he knew how I felt. Didn't want him getting complacent, ignoring the fact that he had to speak to Mum sooner or later. Because, at some point, I was going to lose it. I wouldn't have a choice.

'Me and Charlie are going to spend it together, aren't we?' Dad said.

'How nice,' she answered. She even looked like she meant it.

'Shame this course is taking up so much time, Mum.' I wanted to dare her, make her tell the lie again. 'How long until it finishes?'

'Oh, ages yet. Exams aren't for another couple of months.'

I felt a noose of anger pull tighter round my ribs, then Dad's hand gentle on my shoulder.

But as she stood from her chair I thought I saw tears collect in her eyes. My gaze focused on her and she noticed, trying to stretch her face into a yawn, to pass the tear off as mere tiredness.

There it was. A moment to jump on the rarest of things, a trace of weakness. If I pushed hard enough, or even just told her that I knew everything, then she wouldn't deny it. She couldn't.

My heart pummelled at the prospect, but as the words formed in my brain and marched down to my mouth she turned, a second tear slipping down her cheek. She didn't even bother to wipe it away.

And that was it. All bravery, all momentum gone. I was as weak as her. All I could do was swallow the truth like a sixteen-pound bowling ball and watch her as she gathered her bag and coat.

As the door swished shut, Dad sighed loudly, looking almost as broken as she did.

'Thank you, son.'

'What else was I going to do?'

But I wasn't sure I could do it again. Wasn't sure I could carry another lie. Not when they weighed this much.

I wasn't spending the day with Dad, obviously. I left him venting his frustration on a hunk of meat big enough to belong to a bear, and retrieved my board from under the bush. I wasn't sure it mattered who saw any more.

Throwing it to the ground, my feet on top of it, I pushed hard, feeling the edges of my anxiety peel away. I leapt from path to road, feeling my hopes bounce with the deck as people blurred past. I felt good, alive, calm again.

I hadn't planned a route, or thought I hadn't. But maybe it wasn't a surprise that I found myself on the other side of town, that my left foot didn't stop pushing until the deck jutted up against a set of iron gates, with a sign reading 'Oakview'. Breathing heavily, I rested my forehead against them, looking at the grounds and house behind.

It wasn't like I'd forgotten about Dora completely, although it would've been easy to lose sight of her in all the drama. She'd constantly appeared in my head: her similarity to Mum, but also the differences, just how frail she was, as incoherent as Mum was pushy.

I'd wanted to come back sooner and sit with her again. Maybe there was something she could tell me; after all, she and Mum seemed to communicate somehow. But then I remembered the number of doors to get through to reach her, the nurses and reception staff. It wouldn't be easy to bluff my way past them a second time. Not without Sinus and his iron nerve.

But for once the sun was shining on me, on everything, in fact. The gardens were slowly baking in its heat. There was one spot, by an especially large oak, that shone extra brightly, because I saw a wheelchair parked beside it, a small, creased figure wedged inside. And I knew instantly it was Dora.

I scanned the rest of the grounds, saw a man wearing a dark blue shirt and trousers marching away.

I scanned every metre of the lawn, knowing full well that at any moment Mum could appear, that this wasn't the time for a visit.

Yet somehow, seconds later, I found myself striding across the grass, chest banging harder than it had when I was flying on the board. Maybe I just didn't care any more. Maybe I wanted Mum to catch me. Force the issue. Have it out properly.

I reached Dora just as the guy disappeared. But as I made sure I was on my own, with a look behind me, I tripped over her wheelchair.

To make it worse, I woke her up, a banshee's howl ripping from her lips as her eyes flew open. I tumbled across her lap, trying desperately to make as little contact as possible, and fell to the ground.

Was this how it panned out – arrested for squashing flat

the auntie I never knew I had? Why, when you took my board away, did I have to be so clumsy?

I lay, crumpled, on the lawn, senses unscrambling as I heard a noise.

Not a yelp of pain or distress, but a throaty, rumbling sound. The sort of loud noise that normally accompanied lightning. I looked up from the floor to the wheelchair and saw Dora's head twisted uncomfortably but her eyes dancing, mouth wide open. Her laughter bounced off the trunk of the tree, ricocheting past me and up towards the house.

We must have looked a state: me, lying there grass-stained and wheezing, my board sitting the wrong way up on her lap, wheels spinning gently in appreciation. She looked far more capable of pulling some tricks on it than me.

I chanced a glance over my shoulder, back towards the house, but there was still no one about. I had time, but I had no idea what to ask her, nor what answers I thought I might get in return.

All I could do was start with the blindingly obvious. I was good at that, if nothing else.

'Hello, Auntie Dor,' I grinned, stretching the kinks out of my back. 'Remember me?'

She looked at me hard, eyes squinting, before grinning with the whole of her face.

I might've been wrong, but I could swear she nodded and, anyway, her eyes told me she knew who I was.

I knew I was right to be here. Knew I was right to stay a while. Even if it meant getting caught.

Because my Auntie Dora wanted me here.

31

I spent the best part of an hour sat on my deck by Dora's feet, talking at her like she was my therapist instead of a long-lost relative.

She didn't offer much in the way of answers, but I knew she was listening. Her eyes didn't leave mine, not for a second.

'What I don't get,' I gabbled, well into my stride after an awkward start, 'is why they kept it from me? I mean, it's not like I'm a kid – I'm not going to break into a million pieces just because I hear about you. And as for this whole thing about Mum blaming herself for . . . well, you know. Well, it's rubbish, isn't it? As if I'd believe she hurt you on *purpose*!'

I paused, brain catching up with mouth, wondering whether I'd gone too far, whether she was even managing to follow what I was saying.

'*You* know it was an accident, don't you, Dora?'

I watched intently for a sign, but aside from the tics and tremors that seemed to break across her body at irregular intervals, there was nothing I could be sure about. Other than her eyes, which stayed true and focused. If it was possible for eyes to smile . . . well, hers were beaming.

'I hope you believe me,' I added hastily. 'About not knowing. I don't want you thinking that I was . . . you know, ashamed or anything. That you live here. Because it doesn't bother me. If I'd known, then I would've been down here every week, at least. You know that, right?'

Her left leg shot out from her foot-rest, making contact just below my knee, flush on top of a fading bruise. I tried not to wince. Seemed a bit cheap given the sort of pain she was probably in and, anyway, her face had twisted into the largest, goofiest grin imaginable. It was hard to moan when she looked so joyful.

'I'll take that as a yes,' I added quickly, hearing that chesty laugh of hers rumble up from her boots.

I rambled on less self-consciously after that. About how the news was starting to make sense, in terms of how Mum overprotected me, at least.

'I wish I'd been there, you know. On the day it happened. I know that's a daft thing to say, but it's true, because if someone else had seen the accident then they could have told Mum straight away that it wasn't her fault, just freak bad luck. Dad says the problem now is that she's played it over in her head for way too long, and every time she does, her part in it gets worse. Like she's this killer or something. Mental, I know.'

Dora moaned, long and mournful, an especially wild tic ripping through the entire left side of her body.

'Don't get upset. I'm sure you've tried to tell her enough times. How many arguments has it caused, eh? Because if you're anything like Mum, I'm sure you're happy to stand your ground.'

Another laugh, plus a burning stare, the clearest indication yet that there was a torrent of words that her broken body wouldn't let her deliver.

'It's all right, Auntie Dor,' I added, squeezing her hand as gently as I could. 'You don't have to explain. I understand. I do.'

I didn't know what to say after that: how to move the conversation on, or whether I even should. I worried I was putting unnecessary strain on her. Dad had been pretty straight about just how severe her epilepsy was.

Instead, we sat quietly, saying nothing, her chair groaning occasionally as she wriggled. It wasn't an awkward silence, though. I didn't feel the need to fill it. Instead I watched her, the way her head was so painfully tilted, the way her eyes strained skywards, the joy I thought I could see in them as birds came and went from the oak trees around her. She didn't *seem* to be in pain, and if she was then she must have been an expert in either living with it or ignoring it.

I followed her gaze, trying to see what she saw, and after a few minutes of staring into the swaying branches I felt a calm that was alien to me. So overwhelming that it threatened to have me dozing backwards off my deck. Only a voice cutting clean through the silence had me hopping, shocked, back to my feet.

'Lovely spot, isn't it? Perfect for a nap.'

I had no idea what was going on. For a split second I thought it was Dora: that she'd duped me all along. But as I pulled my blurry gaze back towards her I saw a guy, the same one I'd seen leaving, leaning on the back of Dora's wheelchair. He smiled easily as he draped a cardigan round her shoulders.

What should I say? And how should I say it without looking stupidly guilty?

'Don't worry,' he waved his hand dismissively. 'Ten minutes out here on a day like this? I'd be catching flies too.'

'I wasn't sleeping,' I gabbled, like this was the most important thing. 'I was just . . .'

'I know, resting your eyes, eh? Dora does the same most days, apparently. That right, my friend?' He casually wiped a trail of spit from her mouth. 'Even when she knows there's chores to be done. Them potatoes don't peel themselves, you know? Tom,' he smiled, offering me his hand. 'Agency staff. Filling in for holidays.'

I said nothing. Just gripped his fingers limply and shook.

'This is the bit when . . . ?'

'Huh?' I answered, breaking contact.

'You know, when you answer. Name, number, rank? No pressure, but I think that's how it works.'

'Oh, right, yeah. Charlie.' How stupid? I could have told him any name other than my own.

'And how do you know Dora, then? Family? Boyfriend?' He prodded her shoulder mockingly. 'You dark horse, you.'

'Ha, no, I think I'm a bit old for her. I'm just here on . . .' *Think, Charlie, think.* 'My, er, uncle lives here. Up on the top floor there.' I pointed at the house, like I knew what I was on about. I could've been pointing at the loos for all I knew.'

'Oh, right.' He sounded convinced, but his face wasn't.

'Yeah, I've been visiting for a long time. So kind of know Dora a bit, you know . . .'

'You can tell,' he said, still staring a bit too intensely. 'You look like you've known each other for years.'

There was a pause. I fought the urge to leg it in panic.

'Well, carry on,' he said eventually. 'There's not been a lot of laughs for you lately, has there, Dora? You need someone like Charlie here. Someone who can take you away from this place. Make you think about something new, eh?'

He looked at me, hopefully. 'You can do that, can't you, Charlie?'

I nodded, eyes widening as his words took root in my brain.

I'd come here for answers, but left with something very different. Something far more exciting.

I left with a plan.

32

'That has to be one of the lamest, crazy-assed ideas I've ever heard coming out of your mouth.'

I took a deep breath to stop my ego deflating. It was always a risk asking Sinus for feedback.

'Do you seriously think you can bust your auntie out of hospital and expect to get away with it? What do you think the nurses'll do when they spot you giving her a fireman's lift over the wall? Cos I'll tell you what, Charlie, I don't think they'll come running with a ladder to help you. More likely a straitjacket. And NOT for her either!'

'She's ill, not mad. Plus they don't use straitjackets and you know it.' I tried not to take my frustration out on him, but this idea was all I had. And in my own head I'd convinced myself it was absolutely perfect. Because by pulling it off not only did I show Mum that I knew her secret, and that I was cool with it, but I also made her realize that *my* secret couldn't hurt me either. I mean, think about it. It was win-win-win.

On the day of the Skatefest, all I had to do, with the help of Sinus, was *borrow* Dora from Oakview, just for a couple of hours. Enough time to get her to the park and into the middle of the crowd, which I knew would be huge.

If I could do that and draw Mum to the park too, then I could confront her, show her that I knew everything.

'You have met your mum, haven't you?' Sinus added, another verbal pin stabbing mercilessly into my soul. 'You do remember that she is, how can I put this ... oh yeah, that's it. *A complete control freak*. Do you really think she'll keep a lid on her temper if you pull a fast one in front of everyone she knows?'

'That's just it though, Sinus. Dad says she's more worried about losing face than anything else. She'll hate it, course she will, but you've seen Dora – it's not like she's got three heads or anything. As soon as people meet her, they'll accept her. More than that, they'll love her. And maybe Mum will forgive me for it once she sees that.'

'What, enough to let you march straight on to the top of the ramp? Mate, seriously, you need to have a lie down. Your idea's losing credibility every time your mouth moves.'

'And that's it, is it?' I was gutted now. 'That's your official response? The gospel according to Sinus? Well, if you don't want to help me, mate, on the one occasion that I REALLY need it? Then that's up to you. But I'm doing it anyway.'

He looked at me like I was a loon, his face morphing into the picture of innocence. 'Who said anything about not helping? Your plan might just need some *finessing*. And I do believe I can iron it flat in no time.'

And that was that. The green light was lit, along with a raging fear that spread from my high-tops to my forehead.

*

Sinus was true to his word. Annoyingly. Though I knew that by helping me he was ultimately helping himself too. He was picturing himself with a horde of women on each arm. But for that to happen, and for them to see past his nostrils to the caring soul hidden (deep) within, you were talking about a plan of epic proportions.

The plot developed, though not in terms of busting Dora out of Oakview. I could only presume he was thinking about this while he gave the school the most radical facelift imaginable. Seriously, it was enough to take your breath away.

I don't know how he did it, both in terms of time, and also the amount of spray paint he must've bought, but over the next two and a half weeks he turned every view into a bubble wrap rainbow. His designs were in your face, teasing your eyeballs at every turn. Walls, fences, goalposts, there wasn't a single space Sinus wouldn't dare to tag. And he didn't stop there: instead he went digital too. Every time a teacher turned on a whiteboard there was a 'BWB' shining out of it, information on the canteen's plasma screen was regularly hijacked by him and somehow, best of all, he managed to feed his images into a presentation given by Mr Peach, to the whole school.

'VANDALISM!' the old man yelled. It was quickly becoming his catchphrase. Once more and he'd end up a game-show host instead of a doddery headmaster.

'Some people, the ignorant among us, would dare to call this *art*, to suggest that there is merit to it, when all it does is reduce our buildings, and us in turn, to the lowest of the low. So I'm demanding that you, as responsible members of this school, I'm demanding that you be vigilant, and deliver him or her to me, to be dealt with.'

And with that, he tried to return to his PowerPoint slides, but every time he clicked all that appeared was another gleaming, sleek, jaw-dropping design, each one more dazzling than the last, until, as Peach flicked his controller manically, the roof of the hall threatened to blow clean off with excitement.

I'd never heard anything like it. Never in an assembly, never within the school building, not even when a trainee teacher once inadvertently wore a see-through top during a year nine French exam.

There was applause and cheers, gasps so loud that towards the end I thought we were about to see a standing ovation. And through the noise and the adulation Sinus and I sat, gobsmacked. Well, I did. Sinus wore nothing but his usual smug grin, and his head nodded gently, soaking every bit of adulation up.

The schoolyard buzzed for the rest of the day. Groups assembled in front of the various designs, analysing them, poring over clues about who might have been responsible, what the BWB could possibly mean. Nobody came close, though it made us grin to watch the pencils scribbling on pads, treating it like it was degree level Sudoku.

As the final bell rang, I felt an unusual, unique sensation wash over me. A weird sadness that the day was over. If this was how it was going to be once the Skatefest arrived and our plan paid off, then I had to get practising. I couldn't afford to arse this up, not with this kind of momentum. It simply wasn't an option.

For the next three weeks I burned the candle at both ends. In fact, I spent most of the time twirling it like a flaming baton, without, might I add smugly, ever singeing my fingers. Although I came close on a load of occasions.

There was a lot to do, but no point complaining about it. My eyes never left the gleaming prizes on offer: revenge, glory, girls for Sinus and, most importantly, the chance to cut through the lies that surrounded my family. That alone was worth all the jeopardy.

First of all I attacked skating with venom. There was no point compounding what everyone already thought of me by falling on my back-end at Skatefest. Do that and I might as well not turn up. No, I needed to be sharper than I'd ever been, which meant grabbing every minute, every second, and nailing my technique.

So that's what I did, regardless of the risks of being spotted by Mum in the process. I minimized the chances as best I could, wearing clothes that she wouldn't recognize: baggy jeans plus hoodie belonging to Sinus and a fur-lined Cossack hat with floppy ears that Dad occasionally wore in winter. I might have been sweating like a lunatic in the sun, but it was worth it if it bought me the anonymity I craved.

I hammered the board all over town, knowing I could only hit the ramp after dark, and even then I was reliant on Dad's clandestine help. When I knew Mum was at the hospital, I worked on stamina and balance, weaving in and out of parked cars, zipping around buggies, queues at the bus stop, anything that challenged me to stay on board.

I built up endurance over greater distances too, when Mum was manning the phone at the takeaway and I was out on deliveries. Sometimes it gave me the freedom to hammer it across town to see Dora at Oakview, where I'd sit with her, building up her trust, so that when it came to it, and we did our runner on the big day, she wouldn't freak out. That was something I couldn't afford, not on any account.

The visits became a highlight for me, the moments when I found her waiting on the lawn. I had to be careful: sometimes I only grabbed a minute before spotting a carer returning. But the important thing was that Dora knew I was there, wanting to be part of her life.

I started feeling more confident in her company. The paranoia that I might break her started to disappear: I started to believe, truly, that she was getting something out of me being there.

'We have a laugh, don't we, Auntie Dor?' I asked, as I finished another tale of Sinus's complete lack of tact. She rocked her chair with such joyful force that I had no doubt what the answer was. Made me look forward to introducing them properly; she'd only glimpsed Sinus once as he'd dived into her wardrobe.

'We should have a day out, you know, me and you. Somewhere other than here. What do you reckon?'

She looked at me intently.

'Nowhere far. You wouldn't miss your tea or anything. I just thought you might fancy watching me on this thing.' Her eyes followed towards the board. 'I'm not as quick on these wheels as you are on yours, but I'm up for a race if you are.'

She laughed again and I felt a charge of positivity fizz round my body, reinforcing everything I was trying to do. If Dora was just as up for it as I was, then it had to be worth a stab. Made me wonder if I should enlist more help, maybe from Dad. The thought stayed with me until we were on our own again.

'How well do you know Dora?' I asked him as he drove me home post-practice. I tried to make it sound an innocent question, not wanting to give any hint of my secret visits.

'What do you mean?'

'Well, you know, how often do you see her? Is she comfortable with you like she must be with Mum?'

Dad looked a bit sheepish. 'Well, she knows who I am, but I haven't seen her in months. It's difficult, I didn't know her before the accident and ... well ... I'm not exactly big on small talk.'

'Maybe she doesn't need you to talk to her. It might be enough just to sit and keep her company.'

He looked at me from the corner of his eye, wondering where this new Dora expertise was coming from. I'd pushed too far, too quick.

'Maybe I'll go soon, then. When your mum needs a day off.'

'Or maybe you could do something different with her? I mean, she must get bored with the same surroundings. Might do her good to see something different, something new.'

'Charlie, where are you going with this?'

I shrugged lazily. 'Nowhere. I'm just interested. You can't expect me to know about her, then not care. Be fair, will you?'

'I'll be fair if you tell me the truth. I'm not daft. I can't take her out of hospital just so you can see her again. As much as I know you'd like that, I just can't do it.'

I felt my temper rise. He wasn't going to help my plan in any way, and was also reminding me of the promises he hadn't come good on.

'But you are still going to talk to Mum about everything, aren't you? Like you said you would?'

There was a pause. Not a long one, but it felt definitive. 'I just have to pick the right time.'

'Oh, right. And when is that? When I'm eighteen? Twenty-one? Or are you just going to wait until something really awful happens to Dora? Is she going to have to die before you finally get round to it?'

That hurt him. I know it did, but I didn't flinch. I didn't have time to mess around any more and he shouldn't want to either.

'Look, I'm doing my best,' he pleaded as we stopped at some lights. 'I'm helping you now, aren't I? Isn't that enough?'

I reached for the door handle and pulled it before jumping

out. 'Nowhere near,' I snapped, throwing the deck beneath my feet and pushing off.

'Charlie. Get back in, will you?'

I ignored him.

'Come on. Mum'll be on her way home by now. What if she sees you?'

I smiled thinly. 'Do you really think that matters any more, Dad? Really?'

He had no answer to that, and after crawling alongside me for another hundred metres he accelerated away. I was on my own, in more ways than one.

34

School was buzzing, though it wasn't just the prospect of six weeks off that had everyone so excited. It was the double whammy of Skatefest and Sinus's secret art extravaganza that had everyone whipped into a frenzy.

Mr Peach had been true to his word about the *vandalism* and had done everything in his power to bring the school back to its normal beige tones, short of patrolling the grounds with a rabid Alsatian.

But every time the caretaker painted a wall, Sinus redecorated it, his mind and hand going to extraordinary lengths to ensure the new design was bigger, better, bolder and way more infuriating for the head.

Students started turning up early for lessons, faces pushed through the locked gates for a first peek at the new designs. Copycat images appeared on pencil cases and bags; Peach went ballistic when a huge group of year seven girls stencilled 'BWB' on to their faces in biro. I started wondering when someone would start selling T-shirts, found it hard to believe that Sinus hadn't already thought of it.

He strutted around school, anonymous but strangely famous at the same time (at least in his own head). He spent far less time with his notebook in his hand, which, if the teachers had been smarter, might have given the game away. He didn't seem to miss it; why would he, when he'd swapped a book for canvases that were *way* bigger?

We spent breaks and lunches sprawled in the sun, putting the rest of the plan together as best we could. It was only a week away yet Operation Dora had more holes in it than one of Sinus's hankies. So much so that success or failure rested on life's most unreliable thing: the British weather.

It had to be sunny on the day of Skatefest. If the sun shone, then Dora would be outside; my detailed research into her daily routine told me as much. The equation was simple, warmth plus sunbathing auntie equalled nephew hastily pushing her out of the gates.

But if it was hacking it down, then Sinus and I would have to infiltrate locked doors, CCTV cameras and an army of prying eyes. In short, we'd be stuffed.

We studied as many weather forecasts as possible, poring over long-range possibilities and probabilities, ignoring the doomsayers in favour of those who promised only a twenty per cent chance of rain. Oh my god, we were nerds and we knew it, but for once I really didn't care. Not if it all paid off.

'What's the best thing that could come out of all this?' I asked Sinus, as we lazed, appreciating one of his biggest and funkiest works, a 'BWB' in the shape of a jet bursting clean out of the middle of a fiery sun.

'What, apart from ending up dripping in the fittest women known to humanity?'

'Well, that's a given,' I laughed. 'Love *is* still blind, isn't it?'

He didn't know what I was getting at.

'What else, though?' I went on. 'Apart from that?'

'Not being expelled. I mean, what's the point in redecorating a whole school if you're not there every day to appreciate it?'

'You don't really think Peach will stop painting over them, do you? And as soon as he finds out it's you, you'll be doing it yourself.'

'Nah,' he grinned. 'Never happened to Banksy, and won't to me either.'

'Good to see you setting your standards so high.' It was typical he'd compare himself to the best in the business.

'What about you? Who've you got your eye on? And don't you dare tell me it doesn't matter what happens.'

I thought about it, though my goals weren't as epic as his. A girlfriend would be a big win, but I didn't have the skills or the inclination to juggle more than one. Not that Sinus did either.

An end to all the secrets would be good too, though I couldn't be sure if our plan, even if we pulled it off, would start a new chapter in Mum's honesty. She might think I'd betrayed her as badly as she had me, and if that was the case? Well, we all knew where the power lay in our house. The thought started to suffocate me worse than the bubble wrap ever had.

'I just don't want to be anonymous any more.'

'Anonymous? You? After what already went on with your mum at the ramp?'

'All right, wrong word. I just want it to be *different*, be someone to cheer rather than laugh at. I don't want to be the best, and I don't want to be famous either, I'd just settle for not being infamous. Know what I mean?'

He paused and looked at me momentarily with softening eyes, until . . .

'I haven't got a Scooby-Doo what you're on about. Or why you'd be so modest about it. This is a chance to stamp yourself all over this place, be talked about for years after we've left. Me and you, the comeback kids!'

I shook my head. 'Nah, you can have all that. I'll settle for not doing *the walk* again. If I don't get kicked for the next three years, then it's all been worth it.'

Sinus blew air noisily through his lips.

'I don't know why I waste my talent on you sometimes. Makes me wonder why I didn't choose some other unfortunate to shower with glory.'

'Yeah, I really am lucky, aren't I?' I laced my voice with as much sarcasm as I could muster, but it wasn't enough to penetrate his rhinoceros hide.

'It's my pleasure. You're my project as well as my pal. And to prove it I'm going to need your board.'

'Er, why?' I didn't like the idea of giving it up this close to Skatefest, not when my tricks needed as much work as possible.

'Never you mind why. Just trust your Uncle Sinus. Oh, and you need to think about what to wear on the big day too.'

I looked at my uniform, then thought about my limited wardrobe. 'Well, that's easy enough. Jeans. T-shirt. Probably long-sleeve in case I wipe out spectacularly.'

'You still don't get it, do you?' He was sat up now, eyes

wide and burning. 'I've spent the last month building you the coolest persona in the whole freaking school. Everyone wants to know what 'BWB' means, so when you stand on the top of that ramp, THAT'S the moment everyone's jaw has to drop. That's when they have to realize you're the Bubble Wrap Boy and that you're taking the name back. So if you turn up in jeans and a T-shirt then I'll spray you a costume myself. And you won't look good with a pair of graffiti tits. Believe me.'

Point proved, he lay back, hands behind his head.

Great. Another thing to fill up my brain, alongside kidnap, ridicule and potentially the angriest parents on the planet. It was all going completely to plan. What could possibly go wrong?

35

I should've been nervous the day before I unmasked myself, riddled with doubts about the potential for everything going south, guilty that I was about to pull the fastest trick imaginable on my parents.

But you know what? I wasn't any of those things. I felt like I had momentum, and not just from my wheels spinning faster and faster as I practised.

I'd been pushing myself harder than ever before, cramming every antisocial hour on the ramp that I could. Stepping foot on it at five thirty in the morning should have been painful, but it wasn't. I'd never felt more awake in my life, even after two hours of gruelling drills. By the time I'd done, I'd eaten up every centimetre of the half-pipe, felt like I could scale its heights in a single step if I had to.

Stan, Dan and the others were in for the shock of their lives. I could do this. No doubt about it.

It was a rare thing, having self-confidence and belief. It bubbled so constantly that I was in danger of doing myself damage by holding it in. So I decided to let off pressure with the person who I knew would listen. I went to tell Dora.

Or I tried to. After all, the sun was out, so the odds were I'd find her beneath the big tree, eyes cast skywards.

But when I screeched up to the gates I found the birds soaring unnoticed. Dora was nowhere to be seen.

I thought nothing of it. It wasn't the first time she'd been elsewhere. She could've had a doc's appointment, or physio, or been on a blind date for all I knew, so I pushed on, knowing a bit more endurance work would do me no harm.

Instead I returned an hour later, blinded by sweat and needing a rest in the shade, only to find her spot still vacant. I still had choices. Could give it a while and hang about, or call it quits and surprise her on the big day itself.

Neither option was ideal and my nerves rubbed up against me, reminding me that tomorrow might bring another no-show. And then what would I do? Aside from buying some dynamite and blowing the doors off the place.

Begrudgingly, I made my way home, failing to shake either the nerves or a newfound tiredness out of my limbs. By the time I reached Sinus's, I hadn't the energy to go any further and knocked for him, recognizing his angular silhouette as he came into view.

'Where the hell have you been?'

A typical Sinus greeting.

'You been gargling with acid again?' I asked.

'You were meant to drop it off yesterday,' he continued.

'Drop *what*?'

'What do you mean *what*? I'm not talking about your trousers, you plank. Your board. I need to customize it, don't I? As planned.'

'Oh, right.'

I *had* forgotten, and wasn't that keen to give it up now. The deck and my feet had barely been apart in the last week and the thought of it now made me feel sort of bereft.

'Well, come on then,' he sighed, but before I could even lift the deck up, he ripped it from my grasp and began to shut the door. With me still on the outside.

'Aren't you going to invite me in?' I shouted.

'No chance. You've already set me back the best part of a day and I can't have you distracting me while I work.'

'But what are you going to do to it?'

The door was shut by now, Sinus's next words escaping through the letterbox that I had wedged open.

'We're a team, Charlie, aren't we?' He was walking away, towards his kitchen, shaking a spray can.

'Well, I . . . I . . .'

'There's no I in TEAM, my friend.'

'No, but there is in GIT!' I yelled, as he disappeared from view. 'And don't get any paint near the trucks. If they seize up ahead of tomorrow, I'm done for.'

His voice pealed back, a dismissive 'yeah yeah', before telling me to go home and rest up.

I did as I was told, though it felt like the longest walk imaginable, not to mention the most boring of afternoons.

The flat was empty and no matter what I turned my mind to I couldn't settle. All I could do was play tomorrow's scenarios over in my head in one sickening loop: missing aunties, mobilized police forces and livid parents, but, strangely, not a lot of images of me and Sinus being lifted aloft on the shoulders of a dozen beaming girls.

I tried to take my mind off the premonitions of failure

with some TV, and then a book. Even considered starting some homework before remembering I was supposed to be designing some kind of outfit, which gave me an even bigger case of the fear. I mean, what did Sinus think I was going to come up with?

Was he expecting some kind of superhero suit? Because I didn't think a mask and cape were going to do anything to help my performance. All right, a cape might billow dramatically when I was airborne, but I could also see it getting caught in the trucks and legging me up before I even started. Couldn't imagine it looking so dramatic tucked under me on the stretcher.

Instead I thought about the hard work Sinus had already done and tried to copy his genius on one of my old white T-shirts. The only problem was that he was the design genius, not me, which became evident as soon as the pen made contact with the fabric.

Ten minutes later and I had a design that any six-year-old colour-blind kid would've been proud of – but Dad wouldn't even have used it as a kitchen rag. Embarrassed, I buried it so deep in the bin that not even a bloodhound trained on felt tips could find it.

In the end I found myself turning out every drawer in the flat in the blind hope of finding some kind of inspiration, but aside from a load of soy sauce sachets and outdated menus all I could find was a manky roll of bubble wrap, with most of the pockets popped. It made me shiver to even look at it, but as it was all I had I took it up to my room and laid it beside me on the bed. All I had to do now was work out what to do with it.

But I never did, as somehow, probably due to nervous exhaustion, I fell asleep, waking only when someone hammered loudly on the front door. Startled, I rolled on to the bubble wrap, squeezing out whatever life was left in it, before jumping in shock and whacking my temple on the headboard.

I rolled on to the floor, dazed, hearing ringing in my ears, which slowly changed from a dull buzzing to the endless shrilling of the takeaway's phone.

It merged with the knocking on the door, morphing into the most irritating, discordant piece of dance music I'd ever heard. Seriously, why wasn't Dad answering? He always opened on time, couldn't wait to get in the groove usually, because once the pans were sizzling, he couldn't hear Mum.

Within another minute it was too much to bear, and I crawled to my bedroom door, clocking the time. Ten past five. Ten whole minutes after opening time.

I reached the front door to find three portly, strung-out gents pointing at their watches. They didn't react well to being told we weren't open.

'Gas leak,' I told them. 'Try the chippy on Carr Lane.'

They looked at me with the kind of anger normally reserved for mass murderers or war criminals, before sloping off, shoulders slumped.

Strangely enough, I didn't give them much of a second thought. Instead I went straight for the phone to call Dad's mobile.

Nothing.

So I tried Mum's, which went straight to answerphone.

Madness. We never had family holidays in order to keep

the takeaway open, so for them to simply not show up? Odd.

The next hour saw my paranoia increase as I stewed in the same brew of answerphones, dialling tones and livid hammering on the door.

In the end I taped a 'Closed due to missing parents' sign to the door and hid on the stairs. I took the phone off the hook too, only to worry that one or both of them might be calling me on it.

And once the phone *was* connected again it rang. Course it did. With people selfishly wanting to order food. So I did what any self-respecting kid would do and pretended the line was breaking up, coughing and spluttering until the customers got so cheesed off that they ended up putting the phone down.

It wasn't doing anything for business, but I was beyond caring. Desperate times and all that.

I juggled waiting, calling and spluttering until about eight thirty, when I was on the verge of calling the police, though what I was going to say to them was a bit of a mystery. Not opening a takeaway on time didn't exactly equate to your parents being abducted, did it?

Still, by that point it was *so* out of character that my stress levels were through the roof. With the one finger I had that wasn't shaking, I hit 999 on the landline, and heard, 'Emergency services. Which service do you require?' just as I felt my mobile tremor in my other hand.

The screen said everything I needed it to – *DAD* – so after a garbled 'wrong number' to the operator, I shouted into the mobile.

'Where are you? What's wrong?'

'I'm at the hospital, son. It's not good news.'

I felt my stomach lurch and my head spin, but I forced the words out.

'Is it Mum? What is it? Is she OK?'

'No, no. It's not Mum and not that hospital.' His words got louder, slower, more serious. 'I'm at Oakview, son. It's, er . . . well, it's Dora.'

36

I hammered on Sinus's front door. It wasn't him or the board
I was after, it was his mum.

Her orange face cut through the darkness as the door
opened, and she knew instantly that something was wrong.

'Charlie, love? You all right?'

'I need a lift,' I gabbled. 'I'm sorry to ask, but it's urgent.'

Two minutes later and we were tearing out of their drive
towards town. It would've been quicker had she not wanted
'a moment' to fix her face.

There were a hundred punchlines that could've been
inserted there, most of them revolving around her needing
more than a moment, but even Sinus didn't crack them as
he hurtled down the stairs, hands coated in spray paint.

He could see something was up and bundled into the car
along with us. No way was he missing out, plus it meant he
could fill in the background for his mum. My nerves were
way too tattered to even start.

Dad's call had been brief. Dora had suffered a stroke.
Triggered by a seizure. It was serious. That's why he was
calling. His voice was quiet, echoey, like he was trying to
hide the secret from the corridor in which he stood.

'Does Mum know you're ringing me?'

'No.' I could imagine him looking furtively over his shoulder as he spoke. 'But I didn't know what else to do. The doctors say, well . . . that it's . . .'

I didn't let him finish the sentence. Was grateful that for once he wasn't keeping the big stuff secret. Although my head refused to believe a word of what he was telling me. There was no way it was as grave as he was making out. I mean, she'd hung on for the best part of twenty years, bouncing back from god knows how many seizures. No way she'd give up now. Not when I'd only just met her. Anyone related to Mum was made of stubborner stuff than that.

It wasn't just Dora that I was thinking about. It was Mum too. I had no idea how she'd be coping, had no point of reference when it came to Dora. Could she see this as a blessing, a chance for her to finally get some relief? Somehow I doubted it. From what Dad had said, she'd probably see it as another stick to beat herself with.

I tried to think of what I'd say when she saw me, what I'd do. Would she be so distracted that she'd accept me being there? Or would it just prompt another confrontation, one that I didn't think I could take right now?

I tried to let my head play the scenarios out, but they turned quickly into a jumbled mess that made my panic even worse.

Sinus's mum was hammering the car, but still glanced in the rear-view mirror occasionally, eyes widening as the story unfolded.

'Must've come as a real shock, Charlie.' I hoped she wasn't enjoying the drama as much as she seemed to be, couldn't help but wonder if she'd be on her mobile just as soon as she dropped me off. It wasn't like her and Mum were mates. Fortunately, it was Sinus who stopped me worrying about that, with a rare comforting word.

'It'll all be all right,' he smiled, turning round. 'And don't be worrying about people finding out. We'll keep it quiet, won't we, Mum?'

She flushed scarlet, a new kaleidoscope of colour beneath her neon blusher. 'Goes without saying.' She went back to the road with a newfound concentration that lasted all the way to Oakview's gates.

With a garbled 'thank you' I leapt from the car, feeling the first spots of rain pierce my scalp.

'Do you want us to wait?' Sinus shouted after me.

'No point.' I didn't look back.

I don't know if the rain was an omen, but by the time I reached the doors it was bouncing off the tarmac, hammering the flowers by the door, flattening them to the ground. My first steps on the polished floor sent me skidding into the receptionist's desk, grabbing her attention instantly.

'Can I *help* you?'

Dad appeared quickly over her shoulder and ushered me through the double doors, before folding me into the biggest hug imaginable. I had no idea if it was for my benefit or his.

'I'm sorry,' he whispered, though I had no idea what for, not this time.

'I'm just pleased you called,' I smiled sadly, looking for a sign on his face that things weren't as bad as he'd made out.

'How could I do anything else? I waited as long as I could, but the doctors have said it won't . . .' It was like the words were actually causing him pain. It wasn't like I wanted to hear them either.

'Have you told Mum I'm coming?'

He shook his head, cheeks burning.

'I didn't know how to. How to stop either of you from being hurt any more than you already are.'

'It's all right,' I offered. And it was, sort of. He didn't know how she'd react; I understood that. Now more than ever. 'We'll tell her together, eh?'

We rushed through the corridors in silence, neither of us daring to form any kind of plan. We were going to have to wing it.

As we reached Dora's room, Dad peered through the glass and paused, hand shaking on the panel. Carefully, I moved him to one side. I was all waited out, couldn't put the moment off any longer.

The room was darker than any hospital ward I'd ever seen, the only lights coming from a host of machines that flashed and whirred around the bed. When you added the tubes and wires that draped across Dora, you had a scene of purest science fiction. I couldn't believe that none of the technology had the simple ability to bring her back to us.

I walked slowly. Mum was leaning forward, forehead resting on Dora's twig-like hand. Neither of them was moving.

I'd never experienced anything like this, never had to give the prospect any kind of headspace or thought. And now it threatened to drown me. It was only a supportive, guiding hand from Dad that allowed me to go any further.

My eyes fell on Dora, the pads attached to her chest and temples threatening to dent her already fragile skin. She looked smaller than ever, like the mattress was claiming her centimetre by centimetre, sucking her down towards the ground. I looked for any kind of pain, but couldn't see any. The only sign of life was coming from the machine's pulse rather than her own.

I searched for the right words to let Mum know I was there – but they hid from me. Instead I kept walking until I reached the bed, crouching as I took Dora's other hand in mine.

At first Mum didn't move, probably thinking I was a nurse, but after a while her eyes traced up my hand to my arm, to my shoulder then my face. It wasn't until she'd stared through me for a good few seconds that she realized who she was staring at, and that her secret had collapsed around her.

This was it. There was no going back. For any of us.

37

She said nothing at first, too shocked and appalled at what I was doing there, in her private world. As soon as she saw a fearful Dad, she thought she knew everything she needed to.

'You told Charlie?' she whispered, her voice quiet but laced with bullets. 'He shouldn't be here, not now.'

Dad made a movement forward as his words formed, but I leapt in first.

'I found out.' I said the words forcefully, so there was no doubt. 'Dad told me nothing. Not until I made him.'

It was like I'd spoken in another language. There was no acknowledgement or response; her gaze stayed fixed on Dad, eyes narrowing as she softly laid Dora's hand on the bed. The movement was gentle and precise, her body language anything but.

'How could you?' she hissed hysterically, stalking round the bed towards him. 'I thought you understood. Why I didn't want *anyone* to know. Do you really think Charlie needs to see this? To see what I've done?'

I tried to squeeze between them and break her focus, but as always she wouldn't bend at all.

'You need to listen to me, Mum. It wasn't Dad who told me. It was a nurse on the phone. She thought I was you, and Dad only filled in the rest because I forced him to, because I said I'd go straight to you. He was trying to protect you.'

She finally heard me, eyes widening further as the story fell into place. Taking a slow step backwards, she lifted her hands to her face, like she was too scarred or evil to be seen.

I followed her as she backed away, trying to ease her arms downwards, but her elbows were locked and fingers rigid.

'It's OK,' I told her. 'Really it is. Dad told me what happened.'

'I bet he did.' Her voice was still clear from behind her hands. 'Telling you it wasn't my fault, I suppose. Saying it could've happened to anyone.' She let her hands creep away from her face, revealing the pain screaming from every wrinkle, every tear. 'But it didn't, did it? It happened to me.'

I thought she was going to go on, that the anger and volume would only increase, but as soon as the last word left her, she bit her lip, catching a raking sob as it threatened her whole body. 'It happened to my sister.'

'And it's not your fault, Mum. It was just an *accident*, you must know that?'

'An accident? Is that what you think this is? An accident is smashing a glass or backing your car into a lamp post. Look at Dora and tell me it's the same thing. Look at all these machines and tell me *how* it wasn't my fault?'

But I didn't have time to, because as Mum stopped speaking, Dora's machines took over, their electronic screams clawing at our ears, forcing each of us closer to her bed in panic.

I looked at Dora's face for any sign of pain, but there was none. Her eyelids lay closed, her lips pursed gently beneath the oxygen mask. The machine was the only evidence that inside everything else was failing.

There was a commotion behind us as medical staff raced in, scattering us like nine-pins as they assessed and prodded and touched. I felt an urge to pull them away or tell them to be gentle, but instead held on to Mum, whose limbs seemed to be failing in the same way as her sister's. The staff pressed buttons, changed drips and shot injections, but nothing gave us my auntie back.

Her breathing faded like a dwindling echo; it was as if her bed was on wheels, inching further and further away from us.

I went back to the bed and gingerly took Dora's hand, resisting the urge to talk for fear of sapping the last life from her body. I just hoped she knew I was there: that for once, a first and last time, we *all* were, all her family.

'I'm afraid I don't have good news,' came a voice from behind me. We spun to see a doctor, round-shouldered and stooped, weighed down by years of conversations that started the exact same way.

'The results from the CT scan aren't positive. As feared, Dora's last stroke resulted in a massive cranial bleed. You can see that her body is simply not coping with the trauma. We can make her comfortable and minimize the pain, but aside from that, there's little else we . . .'

I didn't hear the rest.

I knew what was coming, had done from the second I walked into the room, but somehow it still overwhelmed me, sending my mouth into overdrive and my legs into a realm of their own. Mum caught me on the way down, hushing me as another cry escaped.

I had no idea I had that kind of emotion in me. Maybe it was the final snap after all the lies, or the sickening realization that Dora was way more broken than I'd ever realized, but it terrified me that I had the potential to love someone so ferociously when I barely knew them at all. What scared me even more was how I would even start to replace her.

I felt five years old again and looked to Mum, just as I had then. How she was still on her feet I had no idea, but somehow, and with an awful lot of leaning, we stopped each other from crumbling to the floor.

We waited.

And I realized, as the light dimmed around us, that this was the end of a very long wait for Mum. Twenty years of knowing it was coming, of building up to the moment in her mind, all of it wrapped up in your own guilt.

It was too much to get my head around.

In some stupid, naive way, I hadn't considered that Dora might die. Why would I, when all I knew was the gnarled little baby bird that laughed in all the wrong places and charmed everyone she met? She had more life in her than any of the idiots at school.

It was then that the memory of my plan hit me, the stupid, reckless idea to use her simply to serve my own selfish needs.

What would have happened if she'd had the stroke on the way to Skatefest, or in the middle of the crowd? What would I have said to Mum then?

Look on the bright side, Ma. You may have caused the accident, but it was me who actually put her in the ground...

The thought left me cold, the only warmth radiating from Dora's brittle fingers, which I held as Mum busied herself, plumping up pillows and smoothing her sister's hair. Doing, I supposed, the same things she had done for the past two decades. Only doing them at twice the speed, trying to cram as much love into whatever time she had left.

Which didn't add up to much.

We saw midnight come and go in silence, all of us with questions to ask each other. We held them in, though: right now they didn't matter. The only words spoken were to Dora. She was all that mattered.

Was she comfy?

Could she hear us?

I knew we were asking the questions for our own comfort rather than hers, desperately hoping that, wherever she was, she could sense that we were *all* there. That she could slip away knowing *that*, if nothing else.

And when she did finally leave us?

It wasn't peaceful or poignant. It wasn't like it is on the telly or in a book. There were no eyelids fluttering open briefly, no final smile or profound last words.

We only knew she'd gone because the machine told us so with its emotionless wail.

What should have been a final moment of holding her hands tighter, and begging her to come back, was replaced by doctors breaking our grasps, urging us to give them space.

I did as I was told, and stumbled into Dad. Mum did no such thing.

She hung grimly on, tears clinging to her cheeks, no matter how many people came.

She didn't let go or take her eyes off her sister, not even when the doctors finally silenced the whine of the machine, and the room fell quiet.

Instead she sat there, in the same way I guessed she always had.

Except now there was silence.

A silence that none of us felt we would ever fill again.

38

We were told to go home and rest, yet only Dad and I bumped our way home in a cab, the darkness masking our tears.

Mum stayed behind: made it clear there were still things to be done, things she wasn't prepared to wait until morning to tackle.

'She's still my sister,' she'd snapped when Dad tried to persuade her to leave, 'so I still have to do this properly. She deserves that.'

He didn't argue. Course he didn't. He knew one more word would start an avalanche, so after a lingering embrace he backed away.

It was a night for firsts, and a strange moment for me. I couldn't remember the last time they'd ever shown each other that kind of affection. Dad was married to the kitchen, not to Mum – and as for her? Well, I knew now where her affections had been directed all this time.

There would be changes ahead. There had to be, though what they were and how each of us was going to cope with them seemed too much to take in.

'You all right, son?' Dad's hand, although gravel rough, was somehow comforting on mine.

'Is she going to kick off?' I asked, unaware that the question had even been on my mind. 'Tomorrow, when she gets home and it all sinks in?'

His shadow sagged into the chair.

'I've no idea how she'll be, whether she'll react at all. She might be angry, she might be embarrassed that we hid it like we did, that it took someone else to tell you. I just don't know, pal.'

It wasn't like there was a lot of comfort in his words, barely a crumb to seize on, but it was an honest answer at least, one that beat his stock *She's your mum* response. I couldn't help but hope I wouldn't hear that line again.

'I won't know what to say, though. How to bring the whole thing up without upsetting her. Or me,' I said. 'I don't even know if I'm allowed to be mad at her any more. Not now Dora's dead.' I closed my eyes, hoping it might stop the jumble of confusion, but it didn't. Instead my head started to spin like it had when Sinus and me experimented with his mum's drinks cabinet.

'You can feel however you want to, Charlie. You can't hide anything now. There's been too much of that already and look where it's got us.'

'But you saw her when we left hospital. How would she cope if I made the situation even worse?'

'Then bottle it up all you like. Hide it all away and say it's fine, just to protect her. But by doing that, all you're doing is overprotecting her the same way she did you. In the end, all that anger will still come out, even if it's in another twenty years' time. And if you thinks it's messy now, well . . .'

He didn't bother finishing. His logic was already scrapping with all the other stuff my brain couldn't cope with.

All I could do was sit and let the thoughts bounce around, trying to ignore as much of it as I could, hoping that a few hours' sleep might squash some of the paranoia.

But my brain wouldn't rest. I slept, but my head didn't switch off for a second. Instead it took me off in the trippiest of directions. I skated on a board made from Dora's life-support machine, a vicar offering me last rites before pushing me off the top of the ramp. Mum now had tattoos of her sister covering her body; Dad replaced the takeaway with an undertaker's, except the only coffin he stocked was my size, my shape and with my name etched on to a brass plate.

I tried to wake myself, but the dream just laughed and carried on, Dad tipping me into the coffin, cackling as he hammered the nails into the lid.

I woke with a howl, my entire body slicked with sweat.

The banging continued. It was the door downstairs, another unhappy punter, begging for a bag of prawn crackers.

Except it was only nine fifteen. Three hours before Dad usually flipped the sign on the door. I didn't like it, not after yesterday. So I hauled myself down the stairs, whacking myself (as always) on the safety gate.

I didn't know who to expect at the door. My head rampaged on, telling me it would be a copper with more bad news, but instead I found Sinus, arms behind his back, wearing a look of genuine concern.

His mouth opened as I let him in, but no words came out. He looked awkward, fearful almost of what to say, so I saved him the trouble and told him the obvious.

'Dora's dead,' I said, recognizing how blunt and emotionless it sounded. She deserved a better word than that, something longer that explained how brave she'd been. But if that word existed I had no idea what it was, which sent another wave of sadness surging to every corner of my body.

I didn't think I had any tears left, but I was wrong. Didn't think I'd ever show that kind of emotion in front of Sinus, but wasn't in control of that either.

Instead of shifting uncomfortably though, he did a strange and alien thing. He paced forward and took one hand from behind his back, placing it on my shoulder. With his head cocked slightly to one side, and a sad supportive smile on his chops, he did the unthinkable, and said the word I'd never heard him say before, a word I didn't think he knew existed.

'Sorry,' he said. 'Mate, I am so, so sorry.' He pulled me into him, accepting every tear and racking sob that I owned.

We sat in the living room, only moving when the bowl needed more prawn crackers.

'What do they put in these things?' Sinus laughed goofily, a snowstorm of crumbs covering his T-shirt. 'Crack cocaine?'

I laughed, then felt guilty. 'You should ask your Bunion about that. He's the expert these days.'

'True, but I'd happily give him a run for his money.'

It felt good to be talking about something daft, something that didn't set the whine of Dora's life-support machines scratching at my ears again.

And anyway, we'd covered all that off already: Sinus prodding gently, me giving him every bit of detail I could manage without crumpling into a ball again.

'It'll get easier,' he said, though his eyes didn't speak with any kind of authority.

Would it? I wasn't sure I'd be able to find a bit of my brain big enough to hide all my emotions. Not when they ranged from anger to regret to downright filthy bitterness at what I'd missed out on.

'What you need to do is keep busy. Mum reckons that when her dad died it was throwing herself into other things that kept her sane. Gave her a purpose.'

I thought of his mum, of the wall of make-up plastered to her skin, and wondered if that was her grieving mechanism. It made me shudder a bit. No matter how many tips I earned, I couldn't imagine I'd ever earn enough to feed a habit as big as hers.

'And that's where you're lucky, Charlie,' he went on, the smile looking more confident. 'Because you've got everything you need to plough on.' He reached down the side of the settee and with a flourish pulled my deck into view. His smile dazzled on full beam, distracting me from what he clearly wanted me to look at.

I'd forgotten he had the board, to be honest. For the first time in weeks, Skatefest had slipped from my mind, and even with such an obvious prompt it still didn't feel important.

'I would've liked more time,' he said, looking at the underside of the deck, still hidden from me, 'you know, to finesse the design, but I reckon you're still going to like it. It's a limited edition, one of one.' Gripping each end of the board with the palms of his hands, he spun it until the underneath faced me, and finally he had my attention. All of it.

I'd never seen anything to match it. The base shone so brightly that it could've been on fire, the colours so vivid it was like he'd invented new ones of his own. My hands reached forward as if hypnotized, drinking as much of it in as I could without burning my eyes.

It was like he'd used 3D paint. A 'BWB' burst from the wood, each bubble in the design pumped full of air, begging to be popped. I looked closer at the shafts of light he'd sprayed around the lettering, almost gasping as they morphed into flames so red they were scorching the board. But what I loved the most was the nose of the deck, where a tiny figure was clamped on to an oversized board, body stretched into an exaggerated pose as it caught some serious air. The skater was so small that I was in no doubt who it was meant to be, and although I couldn't see his face, there was such joy in the pose that it hit something in me, lighting a spark in my body, a body I thought was too sodden to ever feel excited again.

'That's mental!' I gasped.

'Kind of matches what we had planned then, doesn't it?'

And that was it: the spark fizzled and died.

The board felt leaden and dropped heavily on to my lap.

'What's up?' he asked.

'What were we thinking, Sinus? Did we really believe it was going to work?'

'It was always going to be a bit of a stretch, but it's not like the situation was particularly normal either. Sometimes, I don't know, you just need to take a risk. Even if it means failing.'

'Yeah, well, we don't need to worry about that now, do we? Dora's gone and so the plan is too. I'm grateful, Sinus, really I am. This is just about the greatest thing I've seen in my life. I'm just sorry I'm not going to be able to use it today.'

To me that seemed pretty definitive. A full stop. It wasn't like there was anything to expose any more, nothing to prove.

Sinus thought otherwise, leaping to his feet and arguing immediately.

'You are kidding me, right? What do you mean, you're not going to use it?'

'Calm down, will you? I don't mean *ever*. I just mean *today*. I have to be here, talk to Mum, straighten things out.'

'No, no, no! What you need to do, Charlie, is grow a pair and realize that whatever happened last night doesn't change a thing. You still need to do this!'

I couldn't believe what I was hearing. 'What, so you can impress the girls at school, so you can stand up and take a bow at my expense? Have you got any idea what I had to watch last night? No, course you don't. Nothing registers unless it's all about you, does it? Well, this time, I'm thinking of me for a change.'

He scoffed at me. 'That's crap and you know it. If you

were thinking of yourself, you'd still be all over Skatefest. All you're doing is thinking of your mum, and not upsetting her . . .'

'Her sister just DIED, Sinus!'

'And I'm gutted for her, just like I am for you. But don't you see, Charlie, it might feel like the end of everything, but it's really just the perfect start. Here's your chance to draw a line under everything that's gone on. To turn the hugest negative into a positive SO BIG you won't be able to see the ends of it. Think about it, will you?'

I listened to him, I really did, but I couldn't see how I could do it to Mum, not today.

Strangely he didn't want to hear that either.

'Go on, then. Toss the whole thing away. Doesn't matter to me. My stuff's still up there on the wall, and I don't care if no one finds out today. They will do in time if I want them to.'

He turned to leave, then thought better of it. 'But I'll tell you one thing, whether you believe it or not. I didn't do any of this for me. I did it for you. Because I owe you. It pains me to say it, but it's true. You could've walked away from me loads of times these last few years. I know I've pushed you. Given you hundreds of opportunities, but you never took them. Not once. And here we are now, in a situation we never thought we could ever be in, with the chance for both of us to stand there and say *Oi! Look at us. This is what we can do*. Imagine being able to do that, Charlie. Imagine it. Imagine the look on their faces. Then tell me we'll ever really have this chance again. Because I'll tell you what? If we don't do it now, I don't think we ever will.'

It was a good speech, I had to give him that. The sort of speech that deserved an orchestra swelling in the background. All right, it was manipulative and it might all have been drivel just to get me onside, but he knew me too well.

He'd got me thinking. About where Mum was and when she'd be back. About the fact that I didn't need her to see me on the board any more, at least not today. Maybe today *was* just about the idiots at school, about proving them wrong. Everything else could wait. It had to. My pulse was firing and my feet were itching to jump on the board.

'Maybe we could have a look, you know, at what's going on at the park?'

I never was good at playing things down and Sinus knew it.

'Nice one,' he grinned. 'But you need to sort your clothes out. You won't impress anyone dressed like that.'

Things were changing, or were about to, but it was a relief that some things, the comforting things, always stayed the same.

39

The park was humming: with people, music and the noise of a thousand wheels spinning on tarmac. It was a skater's heaven, even better than I'd dreamed it would be, despite thinking about it for months every time I'd closed my eyes.

The place was transformed. There were food stalls, beer tents and, most importantly, stands where you could buy every bit of skating kit known to man. Tongues were hanging out, wallets being emptied in sheer joy. I took it all in, saw a hundred things I could've bought, but knew I needed none of them. In my hands I had my secret weapon; I knew there wouldn't be a better-looking deck on show all day.

I found it hard to take my eyes off it. Had stared at it for ages back at the flat as Sinus customized the T-shirt I'd chosen to wear; had tripped over several kerbs on the way here due to its seductive qualities.

Sinus was right. It was too good to waste today's opportunity. OK, so the plan had changed, but it didn't matter if Mum missed all this.

In my head it was better now if she didn't see it at all; she'd have enough going on today with doctors and undertakers. I'd tackle her on the subject later, after the funeral, when things were calmer and we were ready to move on.

No, today was the first step, the step that put me on the path: that showed how no amount of humiliation at school would stop me from proving myself. Of proving *them* wrong.

We queued to register for the half-pipe comp, Sinus with his nose in the air for all to see, me with a baseball cap pulled low beneath my hoodie.

If I was going to do this, I wanted to do it with maximum impact, without anyone knowing I was pitching up. Though with hindsight it was a pretty dumb expectation. Unless there was an age category for the under-fives then anyone who saw the short kid in line would know who I was and what I was up to.

'Keep calm, will you?' Sinus hissed next to me.

'I am calm,' I answered, only then noticing the deck shaking in my left hand. 'It's just adrenalin.'

'Yeah, right. Just like the liquid adrenalin dripping down your jeans.'

I knew I wasn't *that* scared, but still chanced a quick look down just in case, which tickled Sinus no end.

'Haven't you got anything else to do?' I asked. 'There must be one wall in this place you haven't violated?'

'*Au contraire*,' he laughed, and pointed at three in our eyeline alone, all daubed with technicolour 'BWB's.

It was all right for him, I thought to myself. He could do his bit at night, under no pressure, with nobody watching him. Unlike me, who had to risk shattering every bone in my body in front of the whole town. They'd forget it if one of his designs was lousy; no way would they afford me the same leniency.

It took longer than it should have done to enrol, not helped by the jobsworth on the desk who was having trouble getting his head around my age. It got so desperate at one point that I thought I was going to have to show him my armpit hair to convince him that I wasn't seven, as he so helpfully believed.

We got there in the end, a maths textbook left in my rucksack just about proving my eligibility, much to the mirth of the floppy-haired kids stood behind us. I didn't recognize them fortunately, nor a lot of the others in the queue, which suited me fine. The further they'd travelled, the less they knew about my past humiliations and the more likely they'd be to accept me solely for what I could do on the board.

We mooched about after that, killing time, watching the other competitions, slack-jawed at the skill on show. It made me twitchy, wondering if I had the skills to be sharing the same air as these lads, never mind skating beside them. Sinus wasn't having a bit of it though, twittering in my ear every time someone pulled off a move.

'I've seen you do that better,' he'd whisper. 'No style, no finesse. You'll kill it.'

I didn't know who this new, improved best mate was, but I knew I liked him. It was like he was sat next to me with a bike pump, blowing as much confidence into me as my body would allow.

It made me itchy to throw the deck beneath my feet and get started, so we headed for the basketball court near the ramp, which everyone was using as a warm-up space for the day. We bundled our way through the crowd, passing more and more of Sinus's designs, so many that they became wallpaper in the world's biggest living room. I felt stupidly lucky that all of this was for me, still found it difficult to take my eyes off them as we moved along.

Which is probably why my clumsy gene took over again, walking me flush into someone coming in the opposite direction. I turned my head towards them to apologize, the words catching in my throat as they came into focus. It was the one person I didn't want to see, whose presence instantly squashed every bit of newfound confidence out of me.

I was doomed.

I'd just walked into Mum.

40

'I think we need to talk, don't you?' she said, face like granite.

'Yes, Mum,' I answered.

Sinus was now cowering behind me, not that I blamed him.

I tried to read something into her words. In some ways they were positive. She hadn't gone mental like last time: there were no raised voices or histrionics, just a disappointed look that said she'd almost expected me to be here.

It wasn't until we headed for the fringes of the crowd that I realized Dad was there too, though he didn't look hacked off either. He looked, I don't know, *poised*. Not something you associated with him unless he had a wok in his hand.

Even when Mum turned to him with the first barbed comment, he didn't lose his cool.

'I should've known something was going on when you suggested the park,' she said, making me want to protect him immediately.

'Look, I'm sorry, Mum. I haven't done this to upset you. I didn't think you'd know, thought you'd be at the hospital still, or sleeping.' She looked like she needed to sleep, her red eyes the only colour on her face.

'I tried to rest,' she answered, 'but my head was full of . . . well, you know. So your dad suggested a walk. I can see why now.'

I had no idea what was coming next. I'd never told Dad about Skatefest, so could only imagine he'd worked out what I was up to over time. But if that was the case, why bring her here? He knew how much the skating meant to me, he'd helped me practise for god's sake, so why grass me up so she could rain on my parade again?

'I don't know what to say to either of you,' she said, tears brewing. 'What sort of sick joke is this? I don't know whether you've done it on purpose or planned it since last night. But I don't want to talk about it here, not in front of your friends, Charlie. You might think I only exist to humiliate you, but it's not the case. You know now why I worry so much. So let's go home. We can talk about it there.'

'Mrs H, please,' piped a voice from behind me. The politest Sinus voice I'd ever heard. 'I know it's none of my business, but you need to see Charlie do this. He's practised really hard, and as much as it pains me to say it, he's got a gift.'

'A gift?' she scoffed. 'Is that what you call it? Well, I've seen him on that thing –' she pointed at the board like it was an enormous turd – 'and I wouldn't call it a gift. I'd call it a death wish. Wouldn't you?'

For some reason, and I've no idea why, Sinus didn't back down at that point. Instead he stepped from behind me and went on.

'I'm really sorry about your sister, Mrs H.' I watched

Mum flinch, then boil as she realized her secret had fanned out further than Dad and me. 'But you have to let Charlie do this. After everything that's been going on at school, this is his cha–'

'Don't you lecture me, Linus.' She managed to shout without raising her voice, which was terrifying. 'Or tell me what's going on for Charlie. Don't you think I know what he's faced at school?'

It was turning into a duel, one in which I could see only one winner, but the prospect of scolded ears didn't bother Sinus a bit. I could see him steeling himself for another verbal volley, before being interrupted by a third, and most unlikely, voice.

'That's just it, love,' Dad interjected, his voice calm. 'You *don't* know what it's been like for Charlie, not really.'

She looked shocked for a second, not used to such a challenge, but it didn't stop Dad.

'I'm no expert either. I only know what I've been told, but I'm telling you, he's been through the absolute wringer.'

'What do you mean?'

'After you confronted him at the ramp, the other kids, well, they didn't make life easy for him.'

'That's an understatement,' scoffed Sinus, who then wilted under stares from both Mum *and* Dad.

'Well, I suppose I could've reacted differently,' she blushed. 'Taken him home instead of handling things there and then. If they teased you as a result, Charlie, then I'm . . .'

'Teased him?' Dad answered. 'Teasing doesn't come anywhere near it,' and with that he launched into the whole humiliation. The videos and photos around school, all building to the grand finale, the bubble wrap debacle. It was weird hearing it: uncomfortable, but not wounding. Like listening to a story that had happened to someone else. I knew where all Dad's detail had come from: Sinus, who else? He shrugged innocently when I looked to him.

As I turned again to Dad, it made me realize what a good job I'd done of bouncing back. Made me realize even more just how important today was in putting things straight, and how completely I was at Mum's mercy.

I wanted to put my hands over my ears as she spoke, couldn't cope with the possibility that she would still frogmarch me home.

'Is this true, Charlie?' There was plenty of doubt in her voice.

'Yes.'

'All of it? Even the bubble wrap stuff?'

I nodded gently, could feel the sweat collect on my back, just as it had under all the layers of plastic.

'So why didn't you tell me? We could've done something about it. Told school. We still can.' She looked around frantically, as if Mr Peach was going to magically appear in the throng, skateboard in hand.

'But it didn't happen at school, Mum. It happened here. And most of the kids aren't even at my school.'

'Then we go to the police. They can't do things like that, it's assault.'

It might have been the grief talking, or sheer undiluted panic, but she had no idea how ridiculous that idea sounded. And I wasn't brave enough to tell her directly. I tried gently to explain.

'But all that would do is set me up as the victim again. Give them every bit of ammo they need to have another pop, and another, and another until I'll never want to get out of bed.'

Sinus could see my bravery growing and stood beside me.

'That's why Charlie needs to get on that ramp today, Mrs H. All he needs is two minutes, two minutes to put an end to it all. Because once they see what he can do, everything changes. Everything.'

Mum was as unsure as Sinus was certain. 'And you can guarantee that, can you, Linus? You can stand there and tell me, one hundred per cent, that every time Charlie takes off on that thing he's going to land on his feet?'

'No, of course he can't,' said Dad.

'Then we go home and we find another way of sorting this out. I can't let you do this, Charlie. I'm sorry. Not today.'

And the tears started again. Bigger and heavier than the night before, ending the game there and then.

'But there won't be another today, will there?' I had no idea where Dad had found his spine, but he certainly had it wedged in good and proper now. 'Because every time something like this comes up, you'll act the same way. You'll find something else, another reason for him not to do it.'

'That's just not true,' she argued.

'But it is. It already is. Look at the trike, for god's sake. He should be delivering on a mountain bike or a racer. In two years' time he should be doing it on a moped!'

That was too much for Mum who'd crossed on to a whole new scale of panic.

'What is it with you?' she cried. 'Can you not understand why I'm finding this difficult? Why, after everything I've let happen in the past, I might want to protect my own son?'

I could see Sinus shifting uncomfortably, looking at his shoes. Even for someone as nosy as him, it was difficult stuff to listen to.

'But we're suffocating him! Both of us. What's going to happen when he turns eighteen and goes to university? What's he going to do when he gets there and has no idea how to cope with anything that happens? We've got to let him make his own mistakes.'

'Oh, it's so easy for you to say, isn't it? But all it takes is one wrong step and that's it.'

Dad changed gear at this point, stepping back from the anger and reaching for her shoulders instead.

'What happened to Dora was a tragedy. A disaster for everyone. But it was a *freak* accident. You couldn't ask a mathematician to give you odds on it happening again. Not to our Charlie. And, besides, I've seen him on this thing. Believe it or not, you might find yourself proud when you see what he can do.'

Mum was flooding by now. Shoulders raised and jerking as she forced words out.

'I don't need to see him on a board for that. I just need him to be careful.'

'And he will be, won't you, son? You've got pads and a helmet, yes?' He shot me a look that screamed, *Please tell me you have pads and a helmet!*

'Elbow, wrist, knees and head. All in my bag. Customized as well, with extra padding.'

'See,' said Dad, relieved. 'Not a thing to worry about, love. You'll see.'

'No, I won't,' Mum answered, a weak smile on her lips. 'You can try all you like to persuade me, but it won't work.' She turned to me, and with what looked like the last bit of energy she had left in her body, said, 'I'm not going to stop you, Charlie. If you need to do this, then go ahead. But I can't watch you do it. I just can't.'

And after a hug that she clearly didn't want to end, she pushed on through the crowd, leaving me completely torn.

'What do I do?' I asked Dad. 'Seriously, what do I do now?'

His reply was certain, emphatic. 'Do what you always planned to, son. Go out there and show them.'

'But what about Mum?'

'She's my concern. Not yours. All you need to do is stay on that board. You hear me? Please?'

And he pushed on too, leaving me alone with Sinus and with a bigger point to prove than ever.

41

It all came down to this. The highlight of the day, the biggest crowd-puller – the half-pipe challenge.

Two minutes to smash as many tricks as possible, with as much grace, devilry and, most importantly, as much air between the deck and the floor. Simple, really, but I worried the only move I had left in me was the one that involved legging it home. Maybe Mum was right? Maybe there *was* another day we could do this.

Fortunately, the devil in my ear refused to let me get away with such a thought.

'Oi!' Sinus spat. 'Don't be wigging out on me now. We're too close. Smell it. Go on, smell it . . .'

My nostrils flared but I got nothing but the fragrance of cheap hot dogs.

'What?'

'That's the last time you'll smell the air without perfume filling your senses. Look around you, Charlie. Girls! They're everywhere.' He had a look on his face like he'd just discovered an untainted hundred-metre-long wall, so I knew what he was getting at. But I didn't see girls. All I saw was a sea of bodies, clamouring for a view of the ramp, knowing they were waiting to see people fail as well as succeed.

I tried to take my mind off the nausea, running through the sequence of tricks I had in my locker, none of them over-complicated, all of them reliant on me using my only real assets, size and speed. To nail both the routine and the crowd's chins to the floor I had to put some serious space between me and the ground, have them reaching for binoculars to pick me out against the clouds. I *could* do it – I'd pulled every single move off in practice – but never back to back. That was the challenge, that was what I *had* to do.

As a thumping bass line kicked in around us, heralding the start of the competition, we felt the crowd around us swell, a surge propelling us forward, a prompt for Sinus to pull me by the hoodie towards the ramp.

'We've got to get closer,' he shouted.

'But I'm number twenty-seven. We've got ages yet.'

To be honest, I didn't want to be that close, not till it was my turn. Didn't think I could hold on to my guts with the other skaters spinning right above my head.

'There's something you've got to see though, pal. My crowning glory.'

Nose first, he ploughed a path to the front, and with a grin and a wave of his arm, unveiled the hugest piece of art he'd sprayed in his life. It covered the entire ramp. But there were no more initials, no more teasing with a simple 'BWB'. Now, it read: *The Bubble Wrap Boy*, each letter popping off the surface, looking like they would be punctured by the gentlest of footsteps.

'No way they're going to forget you now, is there?' Sinus smiled.

If my mind had been crammed with too many conflicting thoughts, it was now full merely of wonder. And it seemed to be infectious. Around me, and on the other side of the ramp, camera phones clicked everywhere. People pointed, mouthed the words and spoke to the person next to them. Shoulders shrugged and eyebrows rose: they had twenty-six skaters to watch until the penny really dropped.

'It's amazing, Sinus.' I thought about shaking his hand, before pulling him into a hug.

'Charlie. You're an attractive man, and I am in the market, but let's face it, it would never work. Your mum would never accept me.'

I slapped his back hard and tried to push Mum from my head, helped by the first skater appearing at the top of the ramp.

I recognized him, a sixth former who'd been there on bubble wrap day, but now, at the top of ramp, confronted with a crowd of hundreds, he didn't look so smug. He looked like I felt – not that I felt sorry for him.

As he pushed off, picking up speed quickly, I didn't wish for him to fall in the clumsy way that he did, but I didn't weep either when he was forced to limp from the ramp, his deck in need of invasive surgery rather than just TLC.

Others came and went in the same way, with differing levels of glory: the crowd rising as one when someone pulled off a storming routine, and wincing together when they went to ground. One poor soul had to be practically scraped off the floor with a spatula after a wipe-out of epic proportions.

Sinus looked aghast: there wasn't space on his design for blood splatters, never mind stray teeth.

Fear rose in me as my time approached. I wanted to fidget and pace, but there wasn't room. Only when skater number twenty-one, Stan, my friend/tormentor appeared at the top, did I decide to watch no more.

'I need to get ready,' I told Sinus.

'Don't forget what I told you to do,' he shouted against the music.

I nodded. His brief was clear. It should've been after the number of times he'd gone over it.

The crowd parted reluctantly, most people not even seeing me as I dipped past at chest level. It didn't help when one woman asked if I'd lost my mum. I didn't bother answering.

Instead, I headed behind the ramp, and with shaking hands emptied my bag of the padding I'd assured Dad I'd wear. There was plenty of it, too, though not as much as Mum had insisted on for that first day aboard the steel rhino.

I didn't forget about the finishing touches that Sinus had demanded either, hiding as many of them as possible beneath my hoodie.

So that was it. I was set. Looking as fat as I was short.

It was an uncomfortable few minutes before they finally called my number, making me feel like a dish on Dad's menu. My head started tricking me with the same old insecurities: what I was doing to Mum, what I'd been prepared to put Dora through. But strangely I wasn't worried about what I was about to subject *myself* to.

A broken arm would heal, and a barrage of abuse was

no different to the norm. Plus, the next few minutes could change all that, as long as I kept hold of myself.

Breathe deep. Look them in the eye. And tell them exactly who you are.

That was what Sinus had told me. That was all I had to remember.

Remembering it at the top of the ramp, though, was a very different matter. It suddenly felt like I was wavering on a cliff edge. Sinus's design seemed to be a million miles away; I had to strain to make sense of the words, when I knew full well what they said.

Matters only got worse when I turned my eyes to the crowd, realizing to my horror that there were way more people there than I'd thought.

They seemed to be swaying woozily, every one of them laughing at the ridiculous sight in front of them.

Some were wondering what mother in her right mind had let her six-year-old kid teeter his way to the top, while others in the know simply howled when they realized who they were looking at. A ripple went round, a cruel mixture of laughter and disbelief.

Only the words of the announcer brought me back to my senses, reminding me of what I had to do.

'Number twenty-seven isn't a newcomer to the ramp, ladies and gents. Instead he's making a glorious comeback after a short, unexpected break from the sport.'

Another laugh from the crowd. More doubt crept in . . .

'So give your support, ladies and gentlemen, for the Pocket Rocket, the Bubble Wrap Boy himself, Charlie Han!'

It had been Sinus's idea to announce the nickname. The big reveal, when the crowd saw the link between the graffiti and the person, the moment when the kids from school, after weeks of subliminal messaging, finally witnessed the penny crash to the floor and saw me in a different light.

And you know what? He was right.

I saw them react, fingers pointed at the ramp and then to me, but now people were smiling instead of laughing. They looked at me expectantly, like suddenly I might be worth watching for a very different reason: one that didn't involve an ambulance.

I couldn't help but look for Dan and Stan, and took pleasure as they shrank before my eyes. I smiled at them before pulling off my hoodie, giving the crowd a flash of my kid-like torso and not even caring. Instead I straightened the bubble wrap bandages covering my elbows and knees, and pulled my T-shirt down, showing the words sprayed on it to every person watching.

Flying for Dora, it read, with a halo replacing the dot above the 'i'. It didn't matter that no one understood what it meant, because *I* did. I remembered how her eyes used to flit across the skies from her chair, watching every single bird that swooped by. And I couldn't help but hope that, somehow, she might be watching in the same way now.

I felt a series of sobs threaten my chest, which exploded into panic, when, in the far corner of the crowd, I thought I spotted her, her piercing brown eyes burning with intensity.

It threw me. I blinked then stared again, heart almost stopping when I realized it wasn't Dora at all, but Mum.

It was definitely her. I recognized the air of panic, could almost hear her stress levels as they fizzed off her. Dad was next to her, arm on her shoulder, exuding everything she wasn't: a calm excitement for what I was about to do.

I stared at them for longer than I should have, ignoring the music that had started, marking my two minutes of glory. I couldn't help it. It wasn't easy to break her grip after fourteen years, even now, even when she was thirty metres away.

The crowd were getting restless – not booing or anything – but I realized I risked losing them. The board nipped at my fingers, reminding me of what I had to do, but I couldn't get Mum's worried face out of my head.

A slow hand-clap started, gathering momentum quickly, until I was full on panicking. My eyes went back to Mum, whose expression mirrored mine. But Dad wasn't flustered. Instead, he smiled supportively and cupped his hands to his mouth, shouting five words with a volume that I never knew he possessed.

'Do it, Charlie. Do it.'

And that was it. It was all I needed. With a roar of my own I threw the deck under my feet and pushed into the void, feeling the wind pick up as the walls blurred. But as the wheels hit the bottom of the curve, I knew my balance was in the wrong place, and as the sky came into view, I felt the board flip from under me, throwing me backwards as it continued towards the clouds.

I braced myself as I tumbled down, no clue where the

bottom was but knowing that its fist was clenched, waiting. Mum flashed into my head, running in slow motion to catch me, not that the image gave me any comfort. There wasn't a person on the planet who could run that quick.

The ramp slapped me hard on the back, my body screaming. I heard my own wail echo back from the crowd and vowed never to move again. I waited for the laughter, but it didn't come. It was like everyone had disappeared. The only thing I heard was the sound of four wheels spinning on wood.

My board rolled against my arm, nestling in my grip. Then there was a shout, a single voice. Sinus.

'Get up, Charlie! Get up.'

And in that second, from nowhere, I felt a jolt of energy, enough to roll me on to my side. My insides groaned, but not enough to stop the spark igniting, and before I knew it, I was on all fours, pushing into my wrists as my knees straightened. My body groaned as I stood, but couldn't shout loud enough to stop my legs from walking towards the slope, deck in hand.

My heart hammered and blood pounded in my ears, but I still heard the crowd. Shouts of encouragement and disbelief, more and more, louder and louder, until their words scrambled into a huge roar of approval that drove me, running, up the ramp wall.

I could've chosen to grab at the ledge and pull myself up, but I hadn't a clue if I had the strength to manage it. So instead, as the wall went vertical, I leapt into the air, planted my feet on the board, and with hands holding those imaginary bags of takeaway food, hoped my balance would kick in.

And it did. The breeze whipped at my jeans as I descended, and although I didn't have the speed to grab any air yet, I knew that with one more shove I'd be exactly where I needed to be. Making myself as small as I could, I tucked into another descent, then straightened as I passed the top of the ramp, the board obediently joining me.

I can't tell you how it felt – there isn't a page big enough to hold the buzz, relief or excitement – but I knew then that momentum was with me. All I had to do was not drop it.

My speed picked up by the second, my confidence accelerating too. I focused hard, remembering what I'd planned, daring to throw my body higher with every single kick-turn.

I started to enjoy myself, grabbing at the board to rotate it as I turned, balancing on one leg, kicking the deck skywards without ever losing control. I knew I was getting some serious air because the crowd were roaring me on, hands in the air when they weren't applauding.

They were all with me, could sense it without even looking down from the top of the ramp.

But it was in that ultimate moment of acceptance I realized that, ironically, it didn't really matter what they thought. I knew what I was doing, and knew I was doing it well. If they wanted to come along for the ride, or slap me on the back afterwards, then fine, but I didn't need their congratulations to know what I'd achieved.

There was a clutch of people, though, whose opinion did matter, and although my time on the ramp was short, I couldn't wait to see what they thought.

So after one last rotation with my arms spread wide, I slid the base of the deck along the ramp edge and skidded to safety. The crowd boomed again, raising a grin the width of my face. But my smile got wider still when I caught sight of Sinus, deep in conversation with a girl beside him. He was pointing at the ramp with one hand, and at a decorated wall with the other. She might have been impressed: it was hard to tell. I had a long way to go until I understood girls the way I did skating. I didn't reckon Sinus would ever be a teacher to learn from either, and I so left him to it.

Instead I searched for my folks through the crowd of raised arms.

I found them eventually: Dad's face was blurred by furiously clapping hands, though I could still make out a smile as he whooped his approval.

But it was Mum's response I really craved. And though her hands weren't clapping and her mouth was closed, I knew I'd made the impression I could only have dreamed of. Because there she stood, arms raised above her head, fingers stretched to the clouds in wonder, as tears of something other than grief slid gently down her face towards her smiling lips.

And that was enough for me.

I must've only had seconds left on the ramp but there was no way I was coming down. Not yet.

I hadn't done enough to win: knew I couldn't, even if I stayed up there for another hour.

But I needed to do it one more time.

So after punching the air in joy, and ripping the bubble wrap off my shoulders and knees, I dropped my body and the board into the void one last time, laughing as the wall rose in front of me, before disappearing.

It wasn't the highest I'd flown, but that didn't matter.

Because, just for a second, as I reached the top of my leap, I thought of Dora, and in that moment, I swear she held me there, before gently letting me fall, back down to earth.

THE END

Acknowledgements

Charlie Han didn't always live above a Chinese chippy. In fact, for a long time, Charlie wasn't Charlie at all. He was Bud Cotton, and he looked like this:

BUD COTTON

I didn't draw this; my pal Boz did, over ten years ago. We worked on *Cotton Bud* for a long time, many drafts, many sketches, but never managed to get him or us into print.

I do need to thank Boz though, for being such a great and supportive friend for the last twenty years. Without his support, I wouldn't have tried to write in the first place.

My thanks also to Jodie Hodges, who I love working (and gossiping) with, and to Caff and Mark Ward, whose skating expertise was priceless.

Ta very much also to the team at Puffin, especially Ben Horslen, who inherited the dubious honour of being my editor (and still managed to smile), Katy Finch for another belting cover and Sam Mackintosh, the greatest copy-editor ever.

Huge thank-yous also to the brilliant Booksellers Crow, The Dublin Davids (O'Callaghan and Maybury), Matthew Williams, Marcus Sedgwick and especially Phil Carroll, who has given me masses of support this last year – what a pal you are.

Finally, a huge thank you to my folks up in 'Ull who support even my craziest ideas, my friends in the Palace who constantly make me grin, and most of all, Laura, Albie, Elsie and Stan, for putting up with me and allowing me to dream. I'm a lucky, lucky lad.

Crystal Palace, January 2014

Sometimes the **fiercest** battles are **fought** at home ...

Turn over for an extract from Phil Earle's

A powerful novel about brotherhood and sacrifice.

Nominated for the Carnegie Medal.

SONNY

Talk is cheap, which explains a lot. Explains why every day of my life has been a shouting match, why, even with the phone held away from my ear, all I could hear was banter. White noise.

We might not have the money for much else, but we can always afford an argument.

The problem was, this noise was stopping me from focusing when I needed to be doing just that. We all stood to cash in here.

My patience stretched tight then snapped. I barked at them to shut up, or words to that effect, and was met by a moment's silence, then . . .

'OOOOOOOOHHH!' Three voices, each one thick with sarcasm. I could imagine them, thirty floors below, all holding imaginary handbags in the air, waving them in my direction, before falling about laughing.

Idiots, I thought, pushing a smile off my lips, before straining back into the distance.

Where is it?

It's late.

I'd been sussing this out for ages, since before Jammy and

Tommo left for Afghanistan. A chance to have some fun and make a bit on the side. Not just for me. For all of us.

But we had to get it right. No mistakes, because whichever way you looked at it, there was risk involved.

I didn't let the thought settle, but not in case it made me change my mind. I mean, it wasn't the first time, or the last either.

It's not breaking the law that gets to me, it's breaking the rules. Jammy's rules.

Never steal from your own.

Sounds like one of the Ten Commandments, doesn't it? Felt like it too, although Jamm has laid down way more than ten over the years. Sometimes I struggle to keep up with them.

But that's the beauty of this scam; we're not breaking the rules. Not really. We're taking, but not from our own. None of that stuff in the van belongs to Mr De Mel till he signs for it. And he won't sign for it, because it won't ever reach him. Not all of it, anyway.

It's a beautiful thing. And it'll work as long as the idiots downstairs manage to keep their minds off passing girls and on the game.

I was starting to twitch: I knew I needed the van soon to keep the lads focused on the plan, so when the silver Transit rolled off the dual carriageway and towards the Ghost estate, I hoped we were in business. A check of the logo on the side – *Fat Barry's Cash and Carry* – and bingo. Game on.

'Right, lads,' the urgency in my voice surprised even me. 'Target is three minutes away. Get in position and stick to what we said.'

A series of whoops and laughter came back, but I didn't have time to wind them in. I had thirty floors to cover before I reached the ground and, unsurprisingly, the pee-stinking lift was still out of order.

By the time I piled through the front door, skipping over a collection of drunks and smackheads, there was no time for even the briefest of pep talks. The van was turning the corner, only thirty metres from the front of Mr De Mel's corner shop. Sucking in a lungful of air, I powered along the kerb, only skipping across the road when I'd passed it.

Look calm.

It wasn't difficult. I wasn't nervous, I was pumped with the knowledge that we could pull it off. Positioning myself a dozen paces behind the van, I walked slowly after it, waiting for it to draw to a halt.

The plan wasn't difficult. Not really. Just needed a bit of play-acting and fortunately we had Wiggy to do that. Never been on a stage in his life, but I swear the boy had movie star written all over him. There wasn't anyone he couldn't charm or scam.

I just couldn't believe I hadn't thought of this earlier.

As the van approached him and slowed, all Wiggy had to do was step into the road, pretending to be drunk. If he timed it right, the impact would be nothing more than a kiss, but with his acting skills, he could turn it into something much more special.

I waited, heart thumping, not daring to look around the vehicle. But then it happened: a thud, the sound of Wiggy's arm slapping the bonnet, a horrendous groan, then shouting from two other voices as the van braked.

Hitch and Den.

Perfect. Their part was simple: turn the drama into a crisis. Make the driver feel so guilty that by the time they'd finished with him, he'd never want to drive again. But most importantly, they had to buy me time.

And that's exactly what they did.

'WHOOOOAAAAH!' shouted Den as he jumped into the road, arms outstretched in panic. His eyes, wide as dinner plates, flitted to Wiggy, who I guessed was writhing about like a fouled centre forward. 'Didn't you see him, you idiot?'

Peering round, I saw the driver's window wind down, then a shaven head emerged to be greeted by Hitch.

'You were driving too fast. It's twenty down here, you know. The kid didn't stand a chance.' It was a bit on the dramatic side, the guy had hardly been racing, but it was enough to get him out of the van to see what was going on under his wheels.

Keeping low to the ground, I scuttled to his door and leaned in to find the keys waiting for me. *Bingo!* Snatching them from the ignition I crept back to the rear, opened the door and jumped in, pulling laundry bags from the waistband of my jeans.

Man, this was way too easy. And inside? It was Santa's grotto. Packed to the rafters with stuff, all of it sellable.

It looked like half of the shops in the city were waiting for a delivery, but that wasn't my problem, and anyway, I couldn't carry it all. All I wanted was the stuff with value, the stuff people on the estate survived on. Booze and smokes basically.

I found the cigarettes quickly, ramming as many as I could into my bags. I reckoned I had a minute, two at the most, before the driver either got fed up or cottoned on. When that happened, I had to be long gone.

Next was the booze, but I had to be picky. Beer was no good, cider neither. Smooth going down, but no resale value. What I needed was the good stuff: spirits. I wouldn't get face value for it, but we'd get a lot more than we would for a four-pack of lager. I found a box of vodka, branded. Perfect. In a bag it went. I had no idea if I'd be able to carry it all but it was worth a go.

It was only when I tried to lift the bags that I realized it was time to leave. With this weight I'd be lucky to waddle across the estate, never mind run. I only wanted one more thing, and paused by the door when I saw them. Grabbing a handful of lollies, I rammed them deep into my pocket, then lowered myself back to the ground.

As I peeled away, I caught Den's attention, and with a smile, he kicked the plan into its closing phase.

'You got a phone, mate?' he demanded of the driver. 'We should get him an ambulance. I don't like the noise he's making.'

I don't know what Wiggy was doing on the ground, but he'd obviously convinced the driver that it was serious. With no sign of complaint, he headed back to his cab, leaving the lads with their cue to splinter.

I took it in from the entrance to our block.

They ran silently, in three completely different directions, Wiggy having made a miraculous recovery from his life-threatening injuries. It was comedy gold – the poor driver returned to nothing but the dust from their heels. All right, he could see the three of them legging it, but hadn't a clue about which one to follow. Instead he swore loudly before seething in my direction. That was my cue to leave too. God knows how he'd react when he saw what I'd been up to.

I climbed the fourteen floors to the flat, barely feeling the weight I was carrying. We'd arranged to meet and split the stuff once the dust had settled, but after dumping the rest of the booty in my room, I slipped two bottles and a carton of cigs into my rucksack. Time was tight and I needed the cash now. It wouldn't take me long to find a home for these.

Back in the sunlight, I peered at my watch then stepped up the pace. Thirty minutes until it all began, and I still had plenty to do.

Fencing the gear took minutes. Two hundred cigs (minus twenty for me, call it commission) to a bunch of lads on the bench, then the vodka to a couple who were already pickled in the stuff, and my pockets were jangling and heavy. I could've haggled for more, but time was tight.

Instead of worrying, I ran over to the centre of the square and the statue, shaking two smokes from the packet as I stood at its feet. Strange, I'd seen these bronze soldiers every day of my life. It was the first thing I saw when I looked out of my bedroom window, but it wasn't till you stood underneath the statue that you realized how massive it was. Beautiful too.

If ever there was a time for speed, this was it. People looked the other way on the estate, did what they had to do to get by. But no one messed with the statue. It was one of the unspoken laws of the place, separating us from the rest of the town, from the people who'd rather we didn't exist. They'd done their best to hide us away from the fancy marina and the fat wallets who threw their cash about on the weekend. It didn't bother us. We'd rather ignore their existence too.

Flicking a look over my shoulder, I sparked up the smokes, dangled them from my mouth and pulled myself carefully on to the plinth. With one foot on the first soldier's knee and a hand on the other's rifle, I hauled myself skywards, stopping when I reached their faces. Gripping hard with one hand, I reached for the cigarettes and pushed them inside each of the mouths till they held.

'Knock yourselves out.' I grinned, wishing I still had a bottle of vodka I could leave them too.

With a jump, I was back on the ground. Resisting the urge to give them a salute, I headed for town. Twenty minutes left and I had plenty of ground to cover.

SONNY

Sweat pooled on my top lip as I ran for the town centre. I licked it away, grimaced, and tried to remember if this was how the sea tasted.

I'd swum in it once, but it was so long back I couldn't recall swallowing any. I remember bobbing next to a piece of used bog paper, but little else. Funny that.

Nerves chewed me as I checked my watch – Dad's watch – a big-faced chrome number that had proved far more reliable than he ever had. It was the only thing he'd left behind. The telly and microwave disappeared with him but Mum never bothered pawning the watch.

'If it was worth anything he'd have remembered it along with the remote control,' she'd said, her words emotionless.

Instead it sat on Jammy's wrist for years, then ended up on mine once he had shipped out. It hadn't left my skin since. Kept my brother close and in my head, despite the miles between us.

It told me I had ten minutes till the parade went through and I still had a stop to make. You didn't turn up without flowers. It wasn't what you did.

Our town had been ordinary. In the dictionary, under

244

that word, there should have been a picture of the place in all its dull glory. In fact, the air base had been the only thing that created a bit of spice. Without the squaddies getting legless and lairy at weekends, there'd have been nothing to put in the local paper. There's only so many car boot sales you can advertise.

Of course, everything changed when the Twin Towers came down. When those planes hit, we felt the tremors all the way over here. We still do.

Suddenly, there were more people in uniform than ever; in town, by the barracks, but especially on the estate: flyering, persuading, filling shaven heads full of dreams. Plenty listened, plenty signed up.

Town got quieter on a Friday night. Our lads were fighting on the other side of the world instead, without the help of booze. It didn't hurt the newspaper though. Columns were filled by the stories of locals coming back broken. Some didn't come home at all.

And that changed everything. Instead of being a nuisance to the town, the air base became this almost holy place. It gave everyone a purpose, because every time a soldier was blown up, they'd parade him through the streets, Union Jack shrouding the fact that inside the coffin bits of him were mangled or missing.

Everyone turned out, the streets were always packed, people came from everywhere, even the south.

The florist had to move to a bigger shop, the undertaker doubled his fleet. The petrol station started selling bouquets of their own, bargain-basement ones that looked like they were already on the way out.

Those flowers died on the forecourt. This wasn't about doing it on the cheap.

My legs twitched as I waited in the queue with a handful of white roses, the ones I always chose out of superstition.

'Lovely choice, darlin',' Mrs Morgan smiled. 'Very tasteful.'

I shoved the money into her hand and broke through the queue behind me; had to be on the lamp post before the trumpeter started.

It took me longer than normal to wade to my space. Two soldiers were coming home today; coaches from Scotland lined the market. Whole communities had come to welcome them back. No one got irritated with me, though. A lot of folk knew my regular spot as I shimmied up the lamp post, wedging my feet either side of the pole. Only when balanced did I retrieve the flowers from the back of my jeans, ignoring the thorns as they dug at my palm.

As always, the clocks chimed before the trumpet cut in and, seamlessly, the hearses crept into view.

It was always this moment that killed me, that stole my breath and mashed my head in total fear.

It could be him. Could be Jamm. I could've missed the phone call or the knock at the door.

How would I ever look Mum or the others in the eye, knowing they'd expect me to step up and be the person he'd been?

I could only ever disappoint them; would only ever fall short of the bloke he was.

I looked for Mum in the crowd, but there were too many

faces, all wearing the same expression. I could picture her anyway, black suit anvil-pressed, hair scraped back precisely with twenty pins. I sometimes wondered if the hair-grips were the only things holding her together.

Her eyes would be scanning the crowd, looking for me. Was I here? Was I all right? Sometimes it felt like she'd never met me. I was hardly made of glass. I *could* get by without him if she gave me the chance.

I didn't let the irritation settle, fortunately didn't have to, as my eyes rested on someone else. And in that moment, none of it mattered, because her eyes found me too. The lines that creased our foreheads disappeared, and although we were separated by hundreds of people and a line of security barriers we couldn't be any closer. It was enough. Had to be.

Only the sight of the garlands through the hearse window brought me back to the street.

Danny

Son

Dad

I allowed myself to breathe when I saw the names on the wreaths clearly, allowed myself a tear as the flowers fell from my hand on to the top of the polished car.

For the past five weeks I'd prayed that I'd never read my brother's name spelled out in poppies.

In the weeks that followed I often wished I had.

SONNY

So you probably want to know who the girl in the crowd was. And that's fine by me. I could talk about Cameron Thompson all day long. Although, inevitably, thoughts of her bring me back to Jammy, and another of his commandments.

Thou shalt not cop off with thy mate's sister.

Keeping to this was proving more difficult than the stealing one.

I mean firstly, they wouldn't have got away with this in Jerusalem or wherever Moses was when his hormones kicked in, and secondly, it was clearly aimed at Cam, as there's only Wiggy who also has a sister.

No disrespect to Tina or anything, but she's . . . ample. So big there's a health warning tattooed under her bra strap about the danger of suffocation.

Don't get me wrong, she's a nice girl, big heart, big everything really, but she's not interested in me, and frankly, phew, ditto and amen to that.

Cam on the other hand is . . . well, it's impossible to explain. She's just Cam.

A stupid, gorgeous, tough, quirky mess of contradictions. People who don't live on the estate would tell you she's typical of a girl from the Ghost, that she's brassy and confrontational. But if you actually watch her, I mean *really* watch her, you'll see that she's never the first to speak. All right, she'll fight her corner if pushed, in fact she's tastier with her fists than any of the lads from the west side of town. But you'll never see her strike first, only strike back.

That's *one* of the things that makes her rock my entire world, but by no means all of it.

I mean, the girl is fit. Tall without being lanky or scrawny, everything in the right place, without her ever feeling the need to flaunt it like others I could mention.

She's everything I'm not, basically, and for that reason I always reckoned she was leagues above me. She's Man Utd to my Grimsby Town. If any of us were ever going to stand a chance with her, it was Jammy.

Which is why the whole thing messes with my head on such an epic scale.

No one knows about it of course. Not Wiggy, Hitch or Den, and especially not Jammy or Tommo. Though if it did get out, the news wouldn't take long to reach them. Ghost estate gossip could easily reach Afghanistan, believe me.

I tried to work out who would be most hacked off if they heard, Tommo or Jamm. Tomm's her brother, after all, so you might say him, but the rule belongs to Jammy, so he'd probably try and come down hard to mark his territory.

I thought about it for a few minutes then gave up. It wasn't like I signed a contract or anything, and I didn't chase it either. These things just happen sometimes. And when they do? Well, you just have to roll with it, don't you?

You see, Cam and Tommo's situation is complicated.

Actually, that's not true. It's not complicated at all, they just have a disgrace for a dad. The kind of disgrace who likes to hide behind his drink; the kind who can't hold his beer by the end of the night, because by then his hands have clenched into fists. Fists he can't straighten out until they've had a go on someone who he's supposed to love.

It's when I see his ratty face that I'm glad I don't have an old man of my own. He'd only disappoint me too.

We've known about what Larry does for years, how he rules the house and how the drink rules him, but it's not like we can do anything about it. Police aren't interested unless someone in the family makes a statement, and the chances of that, knowing the beating that would follow? Well, it's never going to happen.

I often wondered if that was the reason for Tommo joining up. He'd never gone on about the army before. Maybe he'd just had one too many pastings from Larry. I don't mean he signed up out of fear. Tommo wasn't scared of his dad. He'd often take one for the team. Two black eyes and a split lip meant his ma and Cam were left alone. No, he might've followed Jamm because he was about to snap and put the idiot in the hospital. And if he did that? Well, Larry would have no problem dialling 999.

The issue I had with him going to Afghanistan was Cam. I mean, if she was my sister, there's no way I'd leave and put her next in the firing line.

But Tommo had his reasons, and he's sound. One of us. An Original.

On the day he left with the rest of them, I saw his face.

What it meant. I could see some of the other soldiers, all screwed up out of fear for themselves, wondering whether they'd ever come back. I'm sure Tomm was feeling that too. But the way he held on to Cam, the way their bodies shook without a word? It said everything I needed to know, and what I needed to do.

I know what you're thinking when you hear all this. That I engineered it, me and her. But that's not how it happened. First week I dropped her a few texts:

how u doing?

Nothing heavier. Responses were brief.

Fine.
All gud.

Then everything changed with a knock at the door about two and a half weeks in. Listen to me being vague. I know exactly when it was. Eighteen days after they left. It was a Wednesday. Three in the afternoon.

I'd not been in long, still burning up after a run in the heat. It wasn't a clear-your-head-and-keep-fit kind of run, more the if-you-stop-you'll-have-your-head-caved-in variety, but either way, I was sweating. Shirt off and Coke in hand, I'd collapsed in front of the box and was surfing for something to watch. The knock was irritating, but not for long. Not when I saw who it was through the frosted glass.

'Can I come in?' Her words were out before the door was

fully open, before I had time to stick my pecs out and pull my stomach in.

'Course,' I said, resisting the urge to sniff my pits.

'Sorry to barge in,' she went on, turning to face me.

Her cheeks and eyes were red, the top of her chest above her vest was blotchy. Instantly I thought of Larry, of rearranging his face.

'What's up?' I offered her the chair but she wouldn't sit. 'Is it your dad? What's he done?'

Reaching for my phone I scrolled for Den's number. He was the biggest of all of us, the one you wanted at your shoulder when it all went down.

'It's not Dad. I haven't seen him for days. He does this, goes under for a week or so then pitches up like nothing's happened. Longer he's face down in a pint, the better.'

'Then what's up? What's going on?'

Her face dissolved. Not in a pathetic way. She could never be that.

'It's the telly. The news. I've barely switched it off since Tommo went. It's on twenty-four hours. Always about bombs and shootings. I want to turn it off and leave the house, Sonny, but I can't. I keep thinking if I leave it on I'll catch a glimpse of him, and be happy. But he never shows up, and now there's reports of another explosion. One of those improvised ones. The worst yet. Then they said where it was and I couldn't remember if it was the same place that Tommo and Jamm went . . . '

No more words came. She just swayed and looked at me, so scared she couldn't even manage to wipe the smudged tears that fell to the carpet.

I didn't know what to do. Hold her, calm her, stick the news on myself? I daren't do any of them for very different reasons, but had to pick one, so I stabbed at the remote until I reached News24.

As the camera settled on a raging cloud of smoke, I felt nerves prickle across my chest.

It summed up why I'd been resisting the news ever since they left. It was bad enough the scenarios playing out in my head without being confronted with it on the TV too.

I thought about others on the estate going through the same thing. Young mums little older than us, their kids screaming as Daddy left for Helmand. They told me about stuff they did to keep the little ones calm. Jars full of sweets: a Smartie for every day Daddy was away. And when the jar was empty? Then Daddy would be home.

It seemed so simple. Made me wish I was ten years younger and a hundred times more innocent.

It was clearly getting to Cam. She wasn't blinking as she stared at the screen. She didn't even react when the newsreader told us that the family of the blown-up soldier had been informed. All she did was pull the phone from her pocket and jab at the keypad before pushing it to her ear.

'Mum?' Her voice was calmer than when she'd been talking to me. 'Anyone been in touch?'

I presumed the answer was no as she exhaled loudly and slumped on to the settee, hanging up in the process. Immediately I checked my own mobile. Couldn't face the prospect of a missed call from Mum.

'I never understood why they always said that stuff about

families being informed,' she gasped. 'I do now. It's so idiots like me can stop bricking themselves 24/7.' She looked angry at herself, which I wasn't going to have.

'Give yourself a break. It's not easy, I know that.'

'I can't help it, though, Sonny. I can't walk past a newsagent without looking at every page in every rag, just in case I've missed something. If there's a telly in a shop, I'll watch it till the news rolls round to the start again.'

'I understand. I do. But you've got to try not to worry. It's not like we can do anything about it, except trust they'll look after each other.'

I thought for a second that her face had softened from panic to mild dread. But it didn't last long.

'Do you ever find yourself Googling Jamm's name? In case it's leaked on to the web before it reaches the news on TV? I try to stop myself but it's . . . '

'*Hey!*' I interrupted, then let my voice soften. 'It's OK. I get it.' I really did, but had no idea how to make it any easier for her. So I did what I always do and winged it.

'Look at us. All of us, and the scrapes we've got through to be here. All right, it's not easy, but we're still in one piece despite it all. That's why I reckon they'll be all right. There're as many knives here as there are guns over there, and there's none sticking out of us yet, are there? They'll be all right if we are.'

I made a joke of it, patting for an imaginary blade across my shoulders and hers. My fingers turned pure electric as my skin touched hers, especially when she didn't flinch. I left them there, squeezing gently as Jamm disappeared from my head for the first time in weeks.

'And we are all right, aren't we?' she asked, eyes all the more magnetic for the make-up smudged around them.

I felt brave. Don't know why or how, but for once, around her, I felt invincible.

'You tell me? I reckon so.'

And that was it. The gap between us disappeared. Not because I lunged or took advantage. It just happened. And happened. And happened. The footage on the news disappeared. Jamm and Tommo were looking the other way, for now at least.

Breaking a rule had never felt so good.

SONNY

No one knew the estate like us. That's why we were The Originals.

It wasn't a name we bandied about, or sprayed wherever we could.

We weren't a crew, in fact that was the point. We were anything but. An anti-crew.

People talk about living on the Ghost, reckon there's only one thing you need to have straight in your head to survive.

Are you in or are you out?

Know that and you're set.

We knew different. We blew that theory up every day. And, mostly, that was down to Jammy.

He just *got* this place, knew how to play it.

Step in far enough to keep face without ever wading out of your depth.

That's how the commandments came about.

It's not like I don't listen to them or to him. It's more that I could never live up to everything that he was.

Jamm's taller than me. Broader, blonder, better looking, brighter, smarter (there's a difference, apparently), and after a while, standing in that kind of massive shadow gets to you. Stops you even trying to match up. I'm short enough as it is, I don't need people knocking me down any further.

So I play with the commandments. Shave the edges off some, fold others without ever quite ripping them in half.

You see, that's what Jamm isn't always so good at. Being creative.

And that's why no one knows the estate better than me. Because I always need somewhere to hide.

The day after we turned the van over, though, it wasn't just me who needed to be invisible. It was all of us. Seemed like on every pavement there was a sign asking, 'Have you seen these scumbags?'

I was surprised to see them, the signs. They were those Crimestoppers' ones that demand witnesses come forward and spill the beans. They didn't appear very often on the estate. If there was a sign for every shonky deal that went on around here, then we'd be reduced to walking on the roads. Fact.

But for some reason, our little scam had taken the interest of the authorities, or maybe Fat Barry was slipping the coppers a bung to try and get even with us. Either way, we were reminded of our van scam every time we stepped outside. And as a result? Well, I was beginning to feel paranoid. Seemed like it was only a matter of time until someone matched the description on the signs to one of our mugs, and we couldn't have that. It wasn't like I could pay back what I took. The money was already well spent, and to make matters worse, I'd broken another of Jamm's more important rules:

Don't fence goods on the estate.
It's not our patch to sell, only to buy.

Simple, but I'd managed to break it straight after the robbery because I didn't have time to flog my stash anywhere else. Not if I wanted flowers for the parade, and anyway, I was doing that for Jamm. To prove that I'm not as useless as everyone thinks I am.

Except I must be, because I'd sold stuff where I shouldn't have and now I'm paying for it by having to lurk in every alley and staircase on the estate.

I hadn't had to leg it yet, as no one knew it was definitely me. But the lads from the Cuda crew weren't usually bothered with hard evidence. A rumour's all you need when you run practically every racket on the estate.

The prospect of that confrontation, plus the paranoia of the police closing in, was enough to get me calling the boys together, panicking in a way that Jammy never would.

I'd guessed the others had followed the rules and taken their booty clear of the estate before lining their pockets. Then again, I thought, as I opened the door to Wiggy, maybe they had no need to sell their loot at all.

Wiggy's a prolific smoker. One of the best I've ever seen. Can destroy a cig in seconds. Maybe it adds to that movie star demeanour of his, I don't know. I've known him all my life but I can't really remember a time when he didn't have a butt dangling from his lips. Even as he stepped inside now, he had one on the go and a pack tucked into his T-shirt pocket.

Den, however, is more about the sauce. The boy loves a drink. Not in a sitting-on-a-bench-with-a-brown-paper-bag kind of way. We've all seen enough of them, had too many in our families to fall into that trap. What I mean is, if the party needs starting, Den's your go-to guy for a swig of something special.

Not that he turned up today with a four-pack of anything. I think he knew from my message that I wasn't up for a party.

'What's up, then?' he asked, filling the doorway as he entered.

'Give me five minutes and I'll tell you. We're waiting for Hitch.'

He blew a long breath out. 'Be more than five, then.' His face wore a look that said, *I wish I'd brought some beers after all.*

Hitch, you see, well, he's the real Original among us. Like Den, he'll have a go on anything that's getting passed around, but without ever getting trolleyed.

I don't know, he's a quiet one. Keeps it all in. When the banter's flying about, he'll laugh along and point the finger, but it's not often he'll chip in.

We all reckon it's to do with home. None of us exactly come from a model family: any of us that have two parents, one of them's either a drunk or a disgrace. But none of us really know what the score is with Hitch.

I remember asking him, years ago, when we were kids, 'Who do you actually live with?'

He didn't bother to stop chewing his nails as he answered, 'Auntie.'

'Mum or Dad's side?'

'Neither.'

'How is she your auntie, then?'

'Dunno. Just is.'

'Family friend?'

'Something like that. It's complicated.'

That summed him up for me. Hitch was complicated and simple at the same time.

When it all kicks off, he's there. Well, he was. He's seen me through more scrapes than I can remember and never once filled Jammy in on details he didn't need to know.

We just knew to accept whatever was going on behind his front door.

Had our suspicions that he'd mostly brought himself up. Certainly Auntie had disappeared by his seventeenth birthday, leaving him on his own in a shabby council flat. There were times, watching him destroy a bag of chips, that you wondered when the last food had passed his lips. He was an enigma. He came and went. And since Jamm and Tommo had been overseas, he'd been even harder to pin down.

Wiggs sighed after fifteen minutes had dragged by. 'Call him.'

'I already have. Twice.'

'Rudeness.' Den was twitchy too, so when the doorbell buzzed, we were both on the verge of breaking out the party poppers. Can't say Den's delight lasted when I walked back in with Cam, though Wiggs, as usual, led with a gag.

'You done something with your hair, Hitch?'

'Funny you should mention that,' laughed Cam, waving her bag in their direction.

They looked confused as I shot her a look, *I haven't told them yet!*

'What's going on, Sonny?'

'We should wait for Hitch.'

'He's not coming, is he? He's flaked out like always. So let's have it.'

'Ten more minutes . . . '

'NOW!' Den was on his feet, blocking out every inch of sun. I was out of time.

'Well,' I stammered, 'we've got a problem. Or we did have. The good news is I've got a solution. That's why Cam's here.'

They stared at me, then Cam, then me. I saw their hearts sink as they saw the hair clippers come out of her bag.

Wiggy ran his fingers over his skull, looking nothing like his nickname. 'Couldn't you have given me a number one? You didn't have to take the guard off the clippers as well.'

Cam blew the last of the hair away and looked at me. 'Tell the boss, not me.'

'It *will* grow back, you nugget.'

'Not quickly enough,' he moaned. 'It's nearly autumn, you know. I'll have a cold by the end of the week.'

'It'll be far colder in a secure unit if the police catch up with us, so stop your moaning.'

He lit a cig and smoked it sulkily, going on about being too quick to be nabbed for anything.

Dennis, on the other hand, was chuffed with the result, rubbing his fingers through the mohican that Cam had carved him. It was a far cry from his initial anger when I told him the police might be on to us. If he hadn't promised Jamm that he'd keep an eye on me, I'd have been picking my teeth off the carpet for days.

His new fin was wobbly and uneven, but Den was so tall

it was unlikely anyone would notice. 'Smart,' he said, winking at Cam, sending a jolt of jealousy through me.

I wasn't exactly looking my best either, sat on a kitchen stool with a plastic bag tied round my head.

'Can I take this off yet?'

I'd never been bothered about my hair in my life, but suddenly I needed to look at it. Now I had Cam to lose.

She checked her watch and nodded. 'You should be all right. Just make sure you rinse it properly.' I sprinted for the bathroom, hearing her shout, 'And be careful with the towels. Your mum'll kick off if you trash them.'

I did as she told me, not daring to take my head out of the bath until the water ran clear. Only then did I check my appearance in the mirror, a single word leaving my mouth in surprise. It was the same one that all of them shouted as soon as they saw me.

'Jammy!' they said, almost in stereo.

'Up yours! I look nothing like him.'

'Spitting image,' Wiggy laughed.

But it was Cam's reaction that really got to me, despite not uttering a word. All she did was walk towards me and push a hand through my hair. It was a simple gesture, one that had Wiggs and Den looking at each other quizzically.

I should've been concerned that maybe she'd given us away. But I wasn't bothered about that. The only question in my jealous head was this: whose hair did she think she was stroking? Mine? Or my brother's?

Sometimes the FIERCEST BATTLES are fought at HOME

HEROIC

PHIL EARLE

'A war story, a love story, a wonderfully real story' – Kevin Brooks

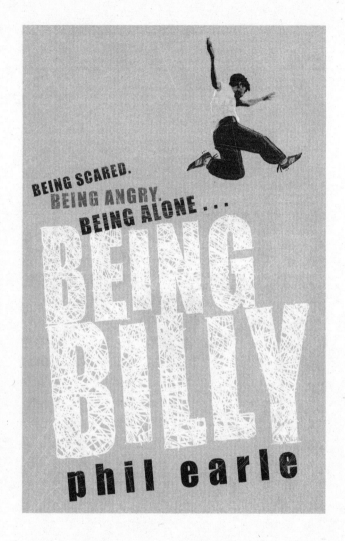

BEING SCARED.
BEING ANGRY.
BEING ALONE . . .

BEING BILLY

phil earle

'Life-affirming, redemptive and really just rather
good' – *Guardian*

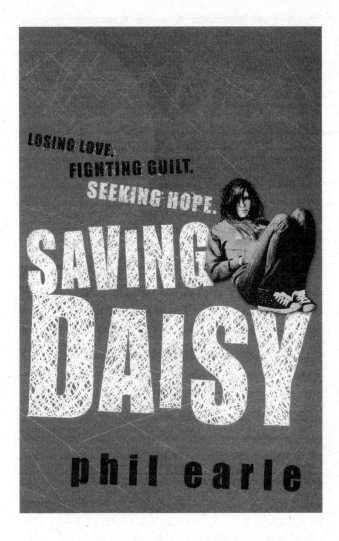

LOSING LOVE.
FIGHTING GUILT.
SEEKING HOPE.

SAVING
DAISY

phil earle

'Phil Earle is capable of portraying the teenage world with
such sensitivity and power that he should be a must-read
author for today's young adults' – *Telegraph*

He just wanted a decent book to read ...

Not too much to ask, is it? It was in 1935 when Allen Lane, Managing Director of Bodley Head Publishers, stood on a platform at Exeter railway station looking for something good to read on his journey back to London. His choice was limited to popular magazines and poor-quality paperbacks – the same choice faced every day by the vast majority of readers, few of whom could afford hardbacks. Lane's disappointment and subsequent anger at the range of books generally available led him to found a company – and change the world.

'We believed in the existence in this country of a vast reading public for intelligent books at a low price, and staked everything on it'
Sir Allen Lane, 1902–1970, founder of Penguin Books

The quality paperback had arrived – and not just in bookshops. Lane was adamant that his Penguins should appear in chain stores and tobacconists, and should cost no more than a packet of cigarettes.

Reading habits (and cigarette prices) have changed since 1935, but Penguin still believes in publishing the best books for everybody to enjoy. We still believe that good design costs no more than bad design, and we still believe that quality books published passionately and responsibly make the world a better place.

So wherever you see the little bird – whether it's on a piece of prize-winning literary fiction or a celebrity autobiography, political tour de force or historical masterpiece, a serial-killer thriller, reference book, world classic or a piece of pure escapism – you can bet that it represents the very best that the genre has to offer.

Whatever you like to read – trust Penguin.